John Warwick Daniel

Character of Stonewall Jackson

John Warwick Daniel

Character of Stonewall Jackson

ISBN/EAN: 9783337065652

Printed in Europe, USA, Canada, Australia, Japan

Cover: Foto ©Raphael Reischuk / pixelio.de

More available books at **www.hansebooks.com**

CHARACTER

OF

STONEWALL JACKSON.

"I AM BECOME A NAME."
Ulysses: TENNYSON.

By JOHN WARWICK DANIEL.

LYNCHBURG
SCHAFFTER & BRYANT, PRINTERS.
1868.

NOTE.

This Sketch of JACKSON is an overgrown Lecture delivered for the benefit of the MANASSAS MEMORIAL ASSOCIATION. It was thought advisable to elaborate the details in preparing it for print, and hence its proportions are enlarged while its original style is retained.

The following volumes have been chiefly relied upon for information:

I. *Life of Lieut.-Gen. Thomas J. Jackson*, by R. L. DABNEY, D.D. Blelock & Co., N. Y., 1864.

II. *The Life of Stonewall Jackson, from Official Papers, Contemporary Narratives, and Personal Acquaintance*, by a VIRGINIAN. Charles B. Richardson, N. Y., 1866.

III. *The Life of Thomas J. Jackson*, by an EX-CADET. James E. Goode, Richmond, 1864.

IV. *Life of Jefferson Davis and Stonewall Jackson.* M. Doolady, N. Y., 1866.

V. *Life and Campaigns of Gen. Robert E. Lee*, by JAMES D. McCABE, Jr. National Publishing Company.

VI. *Army of the Potomac*, by WILLIAM SWINTON. Charles B. Richardson, N. Y., 1866.

VII. *A Memoir of the Last Year of the War for Independence in the Confederate States of America, containing an account of the Operations of his Commands in the years 1864 and 1865*, by Lieut.-Gen. JUBAL A. EARLY. C. W. Button, Lynchburg, 1867.

VIII. *Official Reports of the Confederate States, and United States Authorities.*

STONEWALL JACKSON.

I

THE Caskets in the *Merchant of Venice* that were outwardly attractive were proportionately deceptive. The Prince of Morocco, Portia's first suitor, chose the golden casket, and found in it a death's head. The Prince of Arragon chose the silver one, and was rewarded with the image of a fool. Bassanio selected the modest casket of lead, and within discovered the likeness of his sweet-heart, which was the title to her hand.

The disappointed lovers in the Shakspearian drama were not more deluded by appearances than were the people of the Confederate States in many of the public men to whom they committed their destinies in the late revolution. With the preëminent exception of Jefferson Davis, (by far the greatest man produced on either side,) and one or two others of lesser note, the politicians who figured in the preliminaries of the war proved, like the companions of Ulysses, incapable of directing the winds they had succeeded in arousing. They were, generally speaking, marplots in military affairs, short-sighted and impracticable in finance, and the various other departments of political economy. They were depressed and lost hope with our first serious adversities, and the death's head of a Lost Cause is all that we have gained from their golden promises. A large majority of the military men, in whom it was confidently hoped the South would find great leaders for her armies, were also disappointments. Their course was marked by devoted patriotism and determined valor, and no reproach stains their swords. But with rare exceptions they proved incapable of comprehending the grand proportions and the practical necessities of the revolution, or of combining armies in a wide and complicated field of operations, and the contents of the silver casket were little less in harmony with its shining exterior than were their performances with the expectations they excited.

· It was in a man in whom none imagined to repose the capacities of a great captain, in whom were disclosed those rare martial qualities that best befit the chief of men inflamed with the ideas and passions of a revolution. It was a plain Presbyterian deacon, a professor in a military academy, known hitherto only as a brave subordinate, a conscientious churchman, and an earnest instructor of youth, who rose the most rapidly to high command, who proved most capable of wielding it, who achieved the most brilliant feats of arms, and died the most regretted. And as Bassanio found in the modest casket of lead the talisman of his success in love, so did the people of the South find in the modest person of STONEWALL JACKSON the talisman of their success in war. In his genius was contained the likeness of our victories, and but for the inscrutable Providence that struck him down we would in all probability have found the title-deeds of our independence.

Since the curtain fell after the bloody tragedy of the secession war, every form of intellectual communication has been busily employed to familiarize the world with its actors. Essayists, medalists, lecturers, painters, sculptors and historians have all been tasked to meet popular demands; and amongst their productions we have five histories, and many other lesser delineations of Jackson.

The first of these histories—as they are called by courtesy—is from the Richmond press, and purports to be written by an ex-cadet. Who he may be, we do not know and have no curiosity to know. The book is a small one, and chiefly a rehash of newspaper articles, and has no value as historical authority.

We have then a history of Jefferson Davis and Stonewall Jackson under one cover from M. Doolady, of New York. The volume is written in admirable temper, and with an evident desire for justice. It was intended, however, for current sale, and has no merit as a history.

A life of Jackson, by a Virginian, from Richardson's publishing house, came out in 1866, and the public were falsely assured that it was from the pen of John M. Daniel. This fraud answered its purpose in procuring buyers, and the same work was then republished by Appleton, under the name of its true author, Captain John Esten Cooke. The book is written in a lively, gossipy style, and contains some striking sketches; but it would be a grave misnomer to call it a history.

Dr. Dabney has given us the most elaborate, reliable and interesting treatment of the subject. But it is not a military history in the professional meaning of the term, and such a history was the kind wanted. There is too much of Dr. Dabney's and of General Jackson's religious opinions. Jackson's religious character is inseparable from his military character, and a brief sketch of its striking features would have been in good taste; but the laborious arguments of Dr. Dabney in defence of Presbyterianism, and his strictures upon other denominations, are entirely out of place. Equally ill-timed are the frequent efforts of Dr. Dabney to show that in particular exigencies Providence took particular pains to assist or rescue Jackson and put victory in his hands. Polemics and tactics do not mix well together. Dr. Dabney's theological school is not a place for squad drill or lectures on projectiles, nor a military memoir a place for dissertations on special providences. We believe as firmly in an overruling Providence as Dr. Dabney does. We believe that Providence helps those who help themselves; but as to how or when, that no mortal can say. As the poet has told us, Providence is

" An Isis hid under a veil,"

and, indeed, Revelation itself has said that "its ways are past finding out."

Jackson and his Confederates appeal to a higher tribunal than mere success. As Scott* has tersely put the case, we think that mere victory, as the satirist has said of wealth, cannot be of much importance in the eye of Heaven, seeing in what unworthy association it is sometimes found. Aside from these blemishes of taste, the book is a good one, and so far superior to the majority of war books that it deserves a generous public favor.

The History of Lee, so-called, by McCabe, is valuable only for the portions which the author did not write—the military dispatches and reports. The rest is unreclaimed by a single merit.

---

* Life of Napoleon.

The *History of the Army of the Potomac*, by Mr. Swinton does honor to his head and his heart. It is the best military work that the war has produced. The author has aimed to do full justice to the Army of Northern Virginia and its leaders, and it is equally creditable to him who saw it only from hostile ranks, and to it, "that body of incomparable infantry," as he terms it, that his pen should have pronounced its noblest eulogy.*

General Early's book is in every respect admirable—admirable in temper, admirable in design, admirable in its composition and in its object. It touches only upon campaigns subsequent to Jackson's death, but they were fought often upon the same fields and with the same men, and this volume throws light upon anterior events. Its topographical descriptions are remarkably clear and accurate, and it is a book which may be relied upon. Its author, with a generosity that shines as conspicuously in these self-seeking times as his ability and heroism shone in the war, has donated the proceeds of its sale to the Memorial Associations of Virginia, which have for their object the decent interment of the Confederate Dead. From these sources, from official documents, and from personal recollections of the Army, we shall attempt to present a correct idea of Jackson, and we hope, even in a pamphlet, to produce a true image of his character, as the truth of a likeness does not depend on its size. Had Hæphestion carried out his conception of hewing Mt. Athos into a statue of Alexander his form and features would not have been so well expressed as in the statuette that sits upon the mantel; and our aim shall be to reverse the idea of the ancient artist, and reduce a mass of history into the miniature of a Colossus.

II

THOMAS JONATHAN JACKSON was born in Clarksburg, Harrison county, (West) Virginia, on the 21st of January, 1824. His ancestors were English settlers, who had fixed their residence in that section in 1748. The Jackson family have been distinguished from the first—as far as their record reaches—as people of energy, integrity, courage, and sterling good sense, and it has been frequently and worthily represented in Congress, in the Judiciary, and in the General Assembly of Virginia. When Jackson was three years old, his

---

* Vide see XIII of this pamphlet.

father, who seems to have had but little business capacity, died a bankrupt, and the orphan found an asylum in the home of an uncle, with whom he resided until seventeen years of age. That Thomas generally labored on the farm during the larger part of the year, and learned the rudiments of an ordinary education during the winter months; that he was serious and meditative in his caste of mind, hardy in frame, good natured, resolute, and industrious, constitute the chief facts which the biographers have resurrected from the traditions of his early years. As soon as a hero has made a profound impression on his times, it seems quite easy for his historians to discover in his boyish antecedents the lineaments of the coming man. We are told that Napoleon gave unmistakeable prognostications of Toulon and Austerlitz in laying siege to snow forts and leading forlorn hopes with snowballs during his first winter campaign in boots and breeches. As soon as Clive had finished his daring career in India, all the old folks of his neighborhood in England chatted about the mad-cap pranks of Bob Clive when a boy, and told a wondering world how, to the great terror of all sober-minded people, he used to climb up the steeple of Market Drayton, and nicely balance himself upon the summit. We have all been fully informed by the father of General Grant how distinctly Ulysses' idea of sticking to a bad line, though it took all summer, was prefigured by his sticking to a bad horse in a circus some forty years ago. We have no very significant premonitions of Manassas, and Chancellorsville, and the Foot Cavalry of the Valley, in our hero's youthful amusements, except that he succeeded admirably in mauling rails, while his genius occasionally broke out in a horse race. Dr. Dabney says that it was the gossip of all the countryside that if a horse had any winning qualities in him they would inevitably come out when young Tom Jackson rode him in the race.

As he approached manhood, however, he distinctly revealed those strong qualities which are visible throughout his subsequent career. A great, earnest Englishman* of our own day has justly said, that " sincerity—a great, deep, genuine sincerity—is the first characteristic of all men in any way heroic." Sincerity of purpose, sustained by a never flagging, never hesitating, ever working resolution—sincerity that went forward, and feared not, is the most marked characteristic of Jackson. At about eighteen years of age he resolved to become

---

*Carlyle: Heroes in History.

B

a soldier. He was then without a better education than could be acquired at an old field school; he had little means and few friends; and these discouraged his purpose to apply for a vacant cadetship at West Point. But he had made up his mind, and he answered: "I know I shall have the application necessary to succeed; I hope that I have the capacity; at least I am determined to try.". He finally succeeded in getting an appointment at West Point, and entered the academy in 1842. He barely managed to pass his first examination, but his progress, though slow, was steady and thorough. He made it a rule never to pass over the page of a text book until he had mastered it. He graduated seventeenth in a distinguished class; and such had been his indomitable energy that it was generally remarked that had the course been a little longer he would assuredly have graduated at the head.

In 1846, his novitiate at West Point having ended, he became second lieutenant of artillery in the United States Army.

The Mexican war was then in progress, and he was soon sent to the field as second lieutenant in the light battery of Captain John Bankhead Magruder. In his first fight, at the bombardment of Vera Cruz, his gallantry won promotion to a first lieutenancy. In the second he became a captain by brevet, and when the army entered the city of Mexico he had arisen to the rank of major. In the entire army of General Scott, comprising, as it did, the choice military spirits of the United States, who became the leaders of the armies of the North and South, there was not one who had received more frequent recognitions of merit than this modest lieutenant who had no friends but those of his own making, and had met with no opportunity without improving it.

After the close of the Mexican war he served for several years on garrison duty in New York and in Florida. In 1851 he was elected Professor of Natural and Experimental Philosophy and Artillery Tactics in the Virginia Military Institute. He held that position until 1861, when he left it at the head of the corps of cadets, and never returned until, after signalizing his name and his country forever, he returned upon his bier.

III

Let us glance at some of his prominent qualities as a man before criticising his genius as a General.

Plutarch has observed, in speaking of one of his heroes, that as the expression of the eye often gives us more insight into character than the whole countenance besides, so do incidents and anecdotes reveal more than extended history. There is no character of the war of whom more characteristic incidents are related than Jackson, or of whom the incidents are so characteristic. (He was altogether unique and original, and had more individuality than any man of his times.) He was a man of inflexible qualities. He had neither quickness nor brilliancy of mind, but he was an excellent illustration of the principle that he who can control himself can control others, and his self-control was nearly perfect. By severe discipline he had acquired the power of concentrating or relaxing his energies at will. It was his habit while a professor to spend some hours every night in meditation upon the lessons of the day, and this practice wonderfully developed his memory and his powers of ratiocination. He was never diverted from his studies by the conversation of others, but having once fixed his attention upon an object he was oblivious to all things else until that object was accomplished. His punctuality became a proverb amongst the cadets of the Institute. He slept, studied, and performed all his duties by clock work; and his associates knew the time of day by the movements of Major Jackson. He governed his physical appetites with a rod of iron. Except under medical advice he never touched ardent spirits. To a companion in the army, who invited him to join him in a social glass, he said: "No; I am much obliged to you, but I never use it. I like it, but I am more afraid of it than of federal bullets." "When the people about him," says Dr. Dabney, "complained of headaches or other consequences of imprudence, he would say, 'Do as I do; govern yourself absolutely, and you will not suffer. My head never aches. If a thing disagrees with me, I never eat it.'" He used no stimulants whatever—neither coffee, tea, tobacco or wine, but with rigid simplicity confined himself to the most abstemious asceticism. It was a maxim which he early adopted, and soon illustrated, that "You may be whatever you resolve to be;" and the good sense which preceded, and the stern determination which followed out his resolutions, were sure guarantees of their successful results.

His keen appreciation of, and his warm devotion to principles, indicated a moral nature of the finest and strongest texture.* Perhaps he was more scrupulous about small matters than principle required, but it was because he knew that small defects lead to great vices—that

> "It is the little rift within the lute
> That by and by will make the music mute,
> And ever widening, slowly silence all."

As a professor Major Jackson seems to have discharged his duties with ability and satisfaction, but his reserved manners, his reticence, and his vigorous discipline prevented him from becoming very popular with the cadets, who are always most fond of those genial, sociable natures which mingle most freely with them. He was not fluent, though lucid in his lectures. It is said that in order to acquire facility in lecturing he joined a debating society in Lexington. He was at first very awkward and halting in his efforts, and had frequently to resume his seat in confusion; but he persisted in spite of repeated failures, and became a clear and forcible, though never eloquent, speaker.

In his religious character, Jackson revealed all his earnestness, method, industry, and solid enthusiasm, verifying his professions by his deeds. When his mind was exercised for the first time on the subject of religion, he studied the Bible before he studied any creed— he went to the fountain head of all orthodox religion at once. He then availed himself of his residence in Mexico to become thoroughly acquainted with the doctrines of Roman Catholicism, which pleased

---

* "He was accustomed to argue that having determined any rule to be necessary, he was under a moral obligation to observe it. In vain did any friend plead that the one instance of relaxation in his system could not possibly work an appreciable injury. His uniform answer was: 'Perfectly true; but it would become a precedent for another, and thus my rule would be broken down and health would be injured, which would be a sin.' Thus he carried out his self-denial in the use of his eye-sight so rigidly that even a letter received on Saturday night, if it was only one of compliment and friendship, was not read by him until Monday morning; for his Sabbaths were sacredly reserved from the smallest secular distractions. If his friend exclaimed, 'Surely your eyes would not be injured by the reading of one letter now,' his answer was, 'I suppose they would not; but if I read this letter to-night, which it is not truly necessary to do, I shall be tempted to read something else that interests me to-morrow night, and the next, so that my rule will be broken down.'"—*Dr. Dabney*, p. 75.

but did not satisfy him. He then studied the doctrines of Episcopacy and other denominations, and finally settled into Calvinistic Presbyterianism. He has been called a fanatic in religion, but not justly; for while he was firm to immovability in his own opinions, while he carried his belief in the special interferences of Providence beyond ordinary creeds, he was not only tolerant, but liberal in his views of the religion of others, freely according the right of perfect freedom to their opinions which he asserted to his own. He has been compared to Cromwell very properly, so far as his inflexible abilities for ruling men are concerned, but there was nothing of the puritan in his composition. He was of metal equally hard but more finely tempered in the fires of a purer christianity. He carried his whole soul into the church as into all his undertakings. He instructed a class of young men in Lexington in the evidences of Christianity, and delivered a course of public lectures on the same subject in Beverly, Randolph county, Virginia. He founded and taught as principal a Sabbath school of African slaves, consisting of about one hundred pupils and twelve teachers. Being pleased with the Hebrew system of religious oblations, he scrupulously donated a tithe of his whole income to charitable purposes, besides liberally responding to all special appeals when worthy. His religion tinged all the acts of his life. It was to him the key of the morning and the bolt of the night. It was no shining Sunday garment, but his uniform at home and abroad; his cloak in bivouac, his armor in battle. Frequently, when his army was being formed for battle, his attendants noticed that his lips moved, and his right arm was upraised—they knew that he was in prayer. This done, his resolution was fixed, and execution followed the plan as the discharge of a missile follows the touch of the trigger.

It will be surprising to many to hear that Jackson was a man of the highest ambition. He aspired to eminence in whatever he undertook. He had that thirst for glory which is the almost invariable characteristic of elevated minds, and is inconceivable to all others; and he used every honorable exertion to win it. At the battle of Chapultepec, where his section had lost severely, "his friends asked him if he felt no trepidation when so many were falling around him. He replied, 'No; the only anxiety of which he was conscious in any engagement was a fear lest he should not meet danger enough to make his conduct under it as conspicuous as he desired; and as the fire grew hotter he rejoiced in it as his coveted opportunity.' "* He held that high rank in his profession should be the officer's highest consideration, for which convenience, ease, wealth, and all other personal comforts should be sacrified.† But his ambition was never overweening, envious, selfish, or ill-regulated. To an influential gentleman, who wrote to him for an appointment for a friend during the war, he answered : "If a person desires office in these times, the best thing for him to do is at once to pitch into service somewhere, and work with such energy, zeal, and success, as to impress those around him with the conviction that such are his merits he must be advanced or the interest of the public service must suffer."‡ No fancy, ornamental gentlemen for him! It was by this means that his own ambition sought elevation.

He was no intriguer or office-seeker, but in whatever field he labored he pitched into obstacles with such "energy, zeal, and success" that promotion sought him. His was not the selfish ambition of a Cæsar— "aut Cæsar, aut nullus;" it was not envious like that of Themistocles, whom the trophies of Militiades would not permit to sleep; but like that of Washington, it was inspired by the consciousness of merit, and chastened by devotion to duty. It was not the vain ambition that loved the uppermost places at feasts, or builded the monument for the monument's sake ; but it was the God-given desire to bring to its highest fruition the talent committed to him ; to become worthy of trust over many things by proving faithful over a few; to set his light upon a hill that it might shine before men, and that seeing his good works, they should glorify the Father who sent him.

Jackson's personal appearance sadly disappointed those who had expected to behold the hero of a picture He looked, as he ambled through his camps or his lines on his gaunt sorrel horse, more like a sailor, who had accidentally fallen up, and didn't know how to get down, than like a knightly leader about to perform deeds that song and story would remember. An old faded coat of grey, upon which every season had left its marks, rough boots, a plain military cap, were his constant dress, and no stranger who had met him as he thus attired rode unattended over the battle field, would ever have dreamed that he was "Stonewall Jackson." When he was in Maryland in 1863 a crowd gathered near his headquarters to see him. They

---

*Page 52, Dr. Dabney.
†Page 68.
‡Page 250.

expected epaulets, gold lace, feathers, ornamental aides-de-camp, and numerous interesting items of display. Presently General Jackson stepped out of his tent alone, and told a sentinel to keep the crowd at a distance. "What shabby looking chap is that?" inquired several. "That's 'old Stonewall,'" answered one of his men. "That Stonewall Jackson! Well, I guess he's no great shakes after all," said some of the bystanders; "he's not much for looks any how." You had to come within reach of his eye before you felt the force of his presence. A more resolute, frank, honest, penetrating eye never illumined a human countenance. "When I looked into his face," said a federal prisoner, "my heart sank within me." It was not generally the "blazing eye" which the war writers have spoken of, but there was an expression of inexorable purpose, of slumbering might in it, such as we have never beheld in another.

"A king in the midst of his body guard," says Carlyle,* "with all his trumpets, war horses, and gilt standard bearers, will look great, though he be little; but only some Roman Carus can give audience to satrap ambassadors while seated on the ground, with a woollen cap, and supping on boiled peas like a common soldier." Any military pretender could create a sensation on Pennsylvania Avenue or Franklin Street during the war when duly rigged out with spurs, stars, plumes, and broad cloth—but only such solid men as Robert Lee, Jubal Early, and Stonewall Jackson, could make the faded gray appear grander than royal purple.

IV

It has been a common cry against the officers of the Confederate States Army, who were educated at West Point at the expense of the people of the United States, that "they were taught by the charity of the nation, and that they ungenerously repaid it by turning their swords against their benefactors." The fanatics who urge this argument must be fools "as gross as ignorance made drunk," if upon a cool reflection they do not see its error. The corps of cadets at West Point was composed of appointees made from the several States in proportion to the number of its people, as enumerated for Congressional representation; and although their expenses were paid from the

---

*Essays: Schiller, p. 257.

Treasury of the general government, the means were supplied by taxation of the people of the States—so that each State really supported its own cadets. The southern cadets and army officers withdrew from the pay of the United States simultaneously with the withdrawal of their States from the Union. They were paid virtually by their own States while in public service, and resigned that service the instant that their States ceased to contribute their proportion of public expenditures.

The party in power is now doing us an act of injustice in striking contrast to its false criticisms on our soldiers : taxing the Southern States to educate northern cadets at West Point, and denying entrance to the youths of the South. It is plain, however, that this question, and all similar ones, are involved in the one great issue of the war, " the right of a State to secede." If affirmed, all incidental questions are affirmed. If negatived, all incidental questions are likewise negatived, with neither more or less condemnation individually, than attaches to all.

Jackson was a States Right Democrat, and believed in the right of secession ; but he was never prominently identified with the maintenance of that right until it was committed to arms, and his opinion amounts to no more on that subject than the opinion of any other upright and intelligent citizen. But, however the legal technicalities of secession may be determined, the fair fame of Jackson and his associates in arms cannot be affected. The Declaration of Independence had planted firmly in the American heart, and the " United States" itself traced its legitimacy as a nation to the seminal principle of natural law, that it is one of the unalienable rights of a people to alter or abolish a government when it becomes destructive of the ends it was formed to secure ; and this truth is amply able to sustain the moral weight of the " Lost Cause," if the right of secession were struck from under it. Remitted to our rights as Revolutionists, we point proudly to the Revolution itself. For four years, eight millions of people, poorly provided in every material element of war, defied twenty millions, rich in every resource, and assisted by 300,000 foreign soldiers—beating them back in battle, and yet staining their own hands in no needless blood. Such a struggle could only spring from a great cause. A people could not be exhorted by demagogues to such heroic and such long sustained efforts. It was a revolution of geography, of climate, of blood, of history, of social—not governmental—institutions. A spark kindled it, and it blazed up, a new illustration of the truth well stated by Louis Napoleon in his *Life of Cæsar* : "a great effect is always due to a great cause, never to a small one; in other words, an accident insignificant in appearance never leads to important results, without a preëxisting cause which has permitted this slight accident to produce a great effect. The spark only lights up a vast conflagration when it falls upon combustible matters previously collected."* The election of Abraham Lincoln, a candidate committed to aggressive sectional principles, to the Presidency of the United States, was simply the spark that ignited the vast pile, which, indeed, was almost ready to flame out in spontaneous combustion. Each section instinctively grasped its arms, and the Confederates, having appealed to the "wager of battle," are compelled to abide by its decision. It was intended for, and is in fact, very good satire, but it is also a principle of that practically unprincipled code called International Law, that we find in the lines :

> "Treason ne'er prospers : what's the reason?
> When it does, men dare not call it Treason,"

or as Artemus Ward humorously puts the case, "Traitors are mighty unfortunate people; if they wan't, they wouldn't be traitors." We, as a conquered people, will have to submit to be called traitors until good fortune gives us new names. But our bitterest enemies unconsciously grant that treason washed itself free of every stain, and shone in the spotless purity of honor and of truth, when she grasped the battle flag of the South. "Treason," say they, "must be made odious." Treason stands in history odorous of heroic deeds. Whatever odium may ever attach to it is to be distilled from the venomous lies of odious hearts.

The magazine and newspaper writers of the North generally, have compared what they are pleased to call the "treason" of Jackson and Lee to that of Marlborough and Ney; and some of them seem to imagine that they are excessively generous in elevating the distinguished rebels to the companionship of such mighty names. The cases are not in the least analogous. The ex-officers of the United States Army who espoused the Confederate cause solemnly believed that paramount sovereignty existed in the governments of their States. They declared, in anticipation of war, that in that event they would follow the fortunes of their States. They proclaimed their sentiments openly in the army, while their representatives advocated

---

* Preface to *Life of Cæsar*, by Napoleon III.

C

them in Congress, and such was the legal force of their opinions that those who combátted them in the field have shrunk from discussing them in the courts, even before judges of their own selection. To this day secession has not been decided to be unconstitutional, and our commander-in-chief, the rankest of traitors, if any are traitors, still lies in bonds, enduring, like Paul under the unjust centurion, a judgment which first condemns, then punishes, and finally investigates. The Confederates stand upon firmer legal ground than Washington and his Generals. The latter claimed no right save that which exists in the universal instinct of self-defence, while the former, in addition to their natural rights, were guided by their own interpretation, and a very generally recognized interpretation, of the written law.

Let us glance at the case of Marlborough. He was a major general in the army of James II, when the aggressions of that monarch on the civil and religious liberties of his people caused them to rise in arms against him. In this exigency, Churchhill had the unquestionable right to select which party he would join, and the moralist and the patriot could have found nothing to reprobate in his choice. But he endeavored to serve both masters until he could calculate which was the stronger. He retained his office, and enjoyed its emoluments, but secretly communicated with the Prince of Orange, and schemed against his benefactor. Cæsar was not more unsuspicious of Brutus than James was of his favorite, and Brutus was not more unscrupulous in stabbing Cæsar than Churchhill was in deserting James. The King, so far from listening to the whispers of his attendants against the loyalty of Churchhill, repressed and rebuked them; and when the Prince of Orange had actually landed with an invading army, he promoted him to be lieutenant general, and dispatched him with a corps of five thousand men to meet him. Yet, three months before this, Churchhill had written to William that he was thoroughly devoted to his cause. James, in trusting ignorance of the perfidy of the chief stay of his throne, expected that the next bulletin would bring tidings of his success, and was startled when it arrived to learn that he had deserted, with the Duke of Grafton, and the principal officers of his regiment, to the standard of the invader. By a series of machinations Churchhill succeeded in seducing the monarch's own household and kinsmen from his cause; even persuading the Princess Anne to desert the falling fortunes of her father, and leaving the bereft and desolate king to feel like old King Lear :

> "How sharper than a serpent's tooth it is,
> To have a thankless child."

"My God," exclaimed James, when he heard the news, "my very children have deserted me." Marlborough was simply a bold, brave, adroit, and selfish man, distinguished not more by his brilliant talents as a negotiator and a general, than he is approbious by his low and dishonorable craft. Like Themistocles, he was subtle, sagacious, fearless, and inexhaustible in resources, but like him, also, he disdained the limits that principle sets to action, and applied to measures no other criterion than whether or not they were favorable to his designs.

Marshal Ney's case is a little better. His impulses were good, and we can sympathize with him because he had none of that cold, calculating hard-heartedness that characterized Marlborough. But Ney was a traitor, and though his character may be white-washed with rhetoric, yet the dark color is plainly visible under the white-wash. After swearing allegiance to the Bourbons, he started out from the Tuileries declaring that he would bring back the ex-emperor in an iron cage. As soon as he got to camp he issued a proclamation calling on the troops to desert the Bourbons and mount the tri-color cockade.

Marlborough, as Alison says, betrayed the trust reposed in him by his old master and tried benefactor, to range himself under the banner of a competitor for the throne, to whom he was bound neither by duty nor obligation. Ney abandoned the trust reposed in him by a new master, forced upon an unwilling nation, to rejoin his old benefactor and companion-in-arms.

Neither Jackson, or any of the Confederates betrayed any trust whatever. They acted openly, according to their construction of the Constitution. Marlborough's character wears an ineffaceable stain. Ney's, to say the least, is tarnished by his vacillation. Jackson's was distinguished not more by military ability than by moral worth, and when true history is written his name will be linked in the same bright chain with the names of Hampden and of Washington.

V

In attempting to analyze the military character of Jackson we cannot too carefully guard against those manifold causes which mislead public judgment of military men ; for there is no character so difficult to estimate, or to delineate as that of the military commander. We have seen in our own day so many pretenders made up into heroes by newspaper correspondents and political friends, that we have become skeptical of military fame, and are ready to subscribe to Aristotle's maxim : that the highest wisdom is incredulity—in military affairs at least.

It was remarked by a sagacious French philosopher* that the eulogies pronounced on the Generals of France by members of the Academy would, with a few alterations of names and dates, apply as well to one as to another. And justly—for they were simply rhetorical variations of all the terms of military compliment which their vocabularies furnished, and the figure of the commander was obscured under the profusion of verbose decorations which they heaped upon him. It requires patient research and a keen discrimination to determine in what proportion the victory is due to the genius of the chief, to the ability of his subordinates, to the valor and discipline of his troops, to the character of his adversary, and finally, to those apparent freaks of chance which neither he nor his opponent could foresee or regulate. In considering the campaigns of the most distingushed commanders we frequently find them decided by events which no sagacity could forecast or avert. The sudden swelling of a stream—the stumbling of a horse—the breaking of a wheel—the course of a single bullet—is often the pivot upon which a battle hinges and a continent changes front. Sometimes the wisest dispositions come to grief ; sometimes the most silly result in victory.

Frederick the Great ran away from his first battle and hid in a mill—only to learn, a few hours later, that a tenacious subordinate had clung to the field and changed its fortunes. Thus beginning his career, " covered with glory and corn meal," he became that Frederick whose genius shone so resplendently throughout the Seven Years War, who founded the military power of Prussia, and who Napoleon declared was a super-excellent tactician, and " the most intrepid, most tenacious, and coolest of men."

---

*St. Pierre.

Napoleon maintained at St. Helena that had not the Russian winter been more severe than for many years, he would have held Moscow and been master of the world; and in the single struggle at Waterloo how often does fate seem to defy science, and destiny sport with genius! But for the heavy rain the night before, which soddened the soil and prevented Napoleon from attacking at day light; but for Ney's sending the false intelligence that he had already occupied Quatre Bras; but for the sunken and unseen road of Ohain, which swallowed up the French squadrons; but for the accidental peasant that guided Bulow on the right road; but for the treacherous guide that deceived the Emperor; but for Grouchy's deafness, which prevented his hearing the guns of Waterloo at Wavres; but for the miscarriage of the order sent him to hurry up; but for the Emperor's indisposition on that day—Napoleon had been Czar of Europe—England a province—and the "drama of the world essentially varied in all its subsequent scenes." And see how fate thus conspiring against him seems to waver in his arms. At four o'clock Wellington's right wing is bent back on his centre; Napoleon's glass sweeps over the field; a flash of triumph lights his eye; a conquered world looms up through the smoke; he posts a courier to Paris to say "Waterloo is won." At dark a bewildered, haggard, ruined man is found by his friends on a field near Genappe—a discrowned ruler—a waif of fortune—an imperial fugitive.*

Thus we find the dominion of military glory divided between two monarchs, Skill and Chance—each at times seeming to have absolute sway. No concatenation of favorable circumstances could have produced an Illiad or an Odyssey, an *Ivanhoe* or a *Hamlet*, a code of laws or a steam engine, a picture, or a statue. Apples had fallen for centuries—to none but a Newton did they suggest the theory that governs the universe; to none but a Galileo did the vibration of a chandelier suggest the uses of the pendulum; it was reserved for a Watts to divine the powers of steam from a kettle boiling on a hearth; and for a Franklin to catch the lightnings with a school-boy's toy. Genius alone can win victories in the fields of Literature and Art and Science; but on the field of Mars, Genius seems as often the slave chained to the car of fortune, as the master holding the reins in his hands.

Nor are the results of battles as capable of being as closely

---

* Victor Hugo: Cosette.

examined as the results of other struggles, and efforts. You may read a book over, and over again, carefully subjecting its pretentions to the most searching tests; you may spend hours and days gazing at the picture or the statue, until all the elements of form, color, attitude, and expression have passed in review before a rigid deliberation. But the battle is the thing of the past; no magic wand can reproduce it before you. A mass of conflicting reports meets you, from which the mind can no more reconstruct it than it can conceive the beautiful proportions of a Grecian temple by looking upon a vast heap of rent arches and broken columns. The marks of convulsion are all that is left of it; a moment in which earthquake and thunderstorm seemed to riot together amidst smoke, dust, shouts, blood, groans, has gone, never to return.

Unwilling to patiently untie the knotty mass of facts, the multitude generally cut through it, and say "let success decide for us." "Nothing succeeds like success," was the pithy exclamation of Talleyrand, and we are too often misled by that coquettish nymph,

> "To give to dust that is a little o'er gilt
> More laud than gilt o'er dusted."

When the Knight of the olden time was knighted, it was with the warning injunction to be "faithful, bold and *fortunate*," and "Exitus acta probat" was the inexorable motto by which his deeds were rated

National gratitude and vanity are generally too warm for the formation of cool impartial judgment.

A country in praising its hero, praises itself; its glory and his are one, and it is impossible for it to view with any but partial feelings one whose name is united with victory, and to whom, perhaps, its existence is due. Whether or not he won by real merit, or might have won in half the time, with half the expense, with half as great a loss of men—it does not enquire. He did win! enough! He shall be glorified.

The Northern masses do not remember that Grant poured out blood and treasure in a battle as freely as he would pour out whiskey and water into a cocktail. They do not reflect that any other commonplace piece of stolidity could have done as well with a people as lavish of money, and a soldiery as lavish of blood. They join him in quaffing the intoxicating draught of victory to the health of Uncle Sam—they see not that there is death in the cup!

Our own people were not guiltless of the idolatry of victory.

They abused Sidney Johnston before Shiloh; they wept for him afterwards.

The manifold difficulties in the way of judgment led Marshal Saxe, the Hero of Fontenoy, to declare, " *Toutes les Sciences ont des principes, la guerre seule n'en point encore.*" But to admit such an opinion is to give way to skepticism. A greater than he (Napoleon) tells us, that "all the great Captains of antiquity, and those who in modern times have successfully retraced their footsteps, performed vast achievements only by conforming with the rules and principles of art; that is to say, by correct combinations, and by justly comparing the relations between means and consequences, efforts and obstacles." Closely scanning the history of the campaigns and battles in which Jackson took part, we shall find, we think, that his success was due to an observance of the principles of art, skillfully adapted to the country he fought in, the troops he commanded, the enemy he opposed, and the cause he fought for—in short, by the means to his hand and the obstacles to be encountered.

VI

While alluding to Jackson's other military performances in brief terms, we shall examine his course with critical minuteness only in the first battle of Manassas, and in the Valley campaign of 1862. In the first we see him as a great soldier acting under orders; in the latter he appears as a great General, depending only upon himself.

The morning of the 21st of July, 1861, beheld the Northern and Southern Armies confronting each other with only the narrow stream of Bull Run dividing them. Along that stream the army of General Beauregard was posted in eight brigades, covering the various fords between Union Mills on the right flank, and Stone Bridge on the left —a distance of five miles. Ewell was at Union Mills with his brigade; Jones at McLean's Ford above; Longstreet next at Blackburn's; then Bonham at Mitchell's; Cocke three miles higher at Ball's; while Evans, with eight companies of his own regiment and Wheat's battalion, stood guard at Stone Bridge. General Johnston had already joined General Beauregard with about half of the Army of the Shenandoah from Winchester, including Jackson's brigade; the rest were on the way. Impatient lest Patterson, who had eighteen thousand men with him on the upper Potomac, should unite with McDowell before the coming battle, the Southern Generals had determined to attack the enemy at day.

But during the night the rumble of artillery wheels gave intimations that the enemy were in motion, and at dawn the boom of a heavy gun opposite our left at Stone Bridge announced that McDowell was manœuvering for battle; and the remainder of our troops not having arrived, the Southern Generals determined to await developments. About half past eight o'clock it was discovered that the enemy had made a wide detour, crossed Bull Run two miles above Stone Bridge, and were bearing down on our left flank. With soldierly instinct, Colonel Evans, with 800 men of his little force of 1,100 Carolinians and Louisianians and two guns of Latham's battery, moved to meet this column, and formed his line at the intersection of the Warrenton turnpike and the Sudley road, some twelve hundred yards west of the "Henry Hill," which famous spot is a few hundred yards to the south-east and rear of Stone Bridge. He there met and sustained himself "with skill and unshrinking courage"* against Burnside's brigade, 3,500 strong, which force was a mere curtain to the march of 30,000 men, led by McDowell himself, who were making a still wider circuit to our rear. General Bee, with the seventh and eighth Georgia regiments, the fourth Alabama, the second and two companies of the eleventh Mississippi, were sent to support Evans, and joining him, they held the enemy at bay, until, outflanked and pressed back by dense masses of the enemy, they were forced to retire to the Henry Hill. They were supported in their retreat by the arrival of Hampton's legion, but were followed up rapidly by Heintzleman's and Hunter's divisions, Key's and Sherman's brigades, and more than twenty pieces of light artillery.

General Beauregard had, immediately upon discovering General McDowell's flank movement, ordered his right wing to advance and make a counter attack; but at 11 o'clock, being informed that his order had miscarried, he resolved to meet the enemy on the left, and we now find the columns of both armies drifting toward the vortex of the fiery maelstrom, just commencing to boil on the Henry Hill.

Early in the morning General Jackson had been placed in the rear of Generals Cocke and Bonham in order to support either as occasion might require. At 10 o'clock he had been requested to replace

---

*Johnston's Report, p. 9.

Evans at Stone Bridge, but as he moved to do so, heavy firing in the direction of that officer's new position attracted him; and without waiting for orders he turned his brigade instantly towards it, sent word to Bee and Evans that he was coming, and pushed forward with all possible speed. As his column approached the Henry Hill, the fugitives from the lines of Evans, Bee and Hampton were pouring from it, telling the fugitive's story, not then understood, "they are all cut to pieces;" then came the hobbling and mangled wounded—a seeming verification—while ahead the Hill spouted smoke and flame like a volcano. Amidst such scenes the Virginians moved steadily, with nonchalance and gaiety, joking each other, and picking the ripe blackberries by the way. Jackson at once formed his line under the crest of the hill, with Imboden's, Stanard's, and Pendleton's batteries, twelve guns in all, along his front. The remnants of Bee's, Evans' and Hampton's men rallied on his right, but our line was barely established when the enemy, who had massed their troops upon the hill and concentrated upon it the fire of twenty-four guns, moved forward in a compact mass, got a foothold at the Henry and Robinson houses, crowned the crest with infantry and cannon, and poured into our bosoms a tempest of shot and shell and bullets.

How fitly has it been said that two armies are two wrestlers!* For this little spot of earth the stalwart North and the lithe, active South joined in a death struggle. Within one hundred yards of each other, the opposing batteries blew their hot breath into each other's faces! Every clump of pines, every ditch, every fence sent forth from unseen hands its hissing missiles—the lines writhed, like waves of seething, red hot lava. During all this Jackson kept his brigade lying down, taking the fire but not returning it; but never dismounting from his horse himself, he moved everywhere—an ubiquitous, invulnerable spirit—now directing his gunners, now cheering his infantry. At three o'clock the Federals were gaining ground. Johnston and Beauregard had come—the crisis of the day had come —but our reinforcements—had not come! At this time a shell exploded a caisson of Pendleton's battery, and many horses, breaking their traces, dashed wildly away amidst panic-stricken fugitives. Another shell burst right in the ranks of the fourth and twenty-seventh Carolina regiments, which were formed in double line behind the battery, killing eight men, and horribly mutilating many others.

---

*Victor Hugo: Cosette.

D

Simultaneously, Bee's, Evans' and Hampton's exhausted lines on the right gave way, and the exultant enemy with fresh batteries and regiments rushed over the crest, and seemed about to crush and envelope Jackson's brigade. Bee—his face darkening with the gloom of despair—galloped up to Jackson, and exclaimed: "General, they are beating us back!" Jackson would not be beaten back. He answered: "Then, sir, we will give them the bayonet!" Bee turned to the little squad that still clustered around him, seized a banner, and shouted to them: "There stands Jackson like a stonewall! Rally behind the Virginians! Let us determine to die here, and we will conquer!" Jackson rode rapidly along the front of his men: "Reserve your fire until you are close to them! Rise and charge them!" It was Wellington at Waterloo: "Up Guards and at them!" It was answered likewise. The stonewall had been melted as by electricity into a wave of fire—it rolled into the enemy's centre, consuming battery and line; the hill was cleared, the victory was ours; the artillery captured; the infantry scattered; the back of the anaconda was broken! The enemy reformed afterwards, but too late; for reinforcements had reached us, and soon striking the incoherent mass it dissolved before them, and the rest of the battle of Manassas is a flight from ruin.*

---

* This account of the part taken by Jackson at Manassas does not concur with the official reports or some of the histories. General Beauregard's Report page 31, says that at two o'clock, he gave the order for the right of the line contending for the Henry Hill to advance. To the forces which had been engaged previously, there had been added only the eighth and forty-ninth Virginia Regiments, the second Mississippi, and the sixth North Carolina. He adds: "It was done with uncommon resolution and vigor, and, at the same time, Jackson Brigade pierced the enemy's centre with the determination and the spirit of men who fight for a sacred cause; but it suffered seriously." General B. states that the enemy rallied soon however, "recovered their ground and guns, and renewed the offensive."

In the latter assertion, I am satisfied from recollection, and from concurrent opinions of others there, that he is mistaken. The Henry Hill was never regained after Jackson carried it. General Beauregard says at about three o'clock he ordered a second effort to carry the Hill—that the attack was general, and the whole ground swept clear of the enemy, and the plateau around the Henry and Robinson houses finally in our possession. In this last attack all the additional regiments that had reached the field, participated, and Smith and Early, arriving on the enemy's left and rear just after it, followed up and secured its fruits.

The Robinson house, which is three hundred yards north of the Henry Hill, may have changed hands as often as General B. states, and doubtless

The great Condé said of William of Orange, after the bloody day of Seneff, that he bore himself in all respects like an old General, except in exposing himself like a young soldier. With a musket ball in one hand and the blood streaming over his cuirass, he would press into the very thickest of the fray, mindful only of victory.

The remark is literally and entirely applicable to Jackson at Manassas. He had shown the cool judgment of an old General in going to sustain an important point without orders; in forming his brigade deliberately under fire, and giving it time to rest before charging; in holding it in check for two hours until he saw that the moment for action had arrived; in embracing that moment without hesitation, and animating all to improve it. Pierced through the hand with a bullet during the fight, he had not paused for a moment even to bind the wound, but with all the enthusiasm of a young soldier he had been everywhere that the battle raged hottest, inspiring the weak-hearted and strengthening the strong with his presence. His brigade had been worthy of its commander. It had marched forty miles in less than twenty-four hours to get to the battle-field ; after a short rest it had been double-quicked into fire ; it had withstood fire for two hours without returning it, and it had lost five hundred out of its twenty-five hundred brave men. But it had won an imperishable name. Bee, inspired by its commander, had baptized it with his last words in immortality. It stands in history as the "Stonewall Brigade," and the storms of ages will beat in vain against that heroic rock of the battle ocean, which dashed into spray so often the waves of federal fire.

VII

After the battle General Jackson ardently desired to push the enemy and essay the capture of Washington, but the Confederate Generals Johnston and Beauregard concluded to do nothing, and there was inaugurated that fatal policy of inactivity which had its sequel at Appomattox Court-House. General Jackson was not called

---

did—but the Henry House remained in our hands after being taken. Perhaps this error arose from the fact that before the charge of Jackson's Brigade, one of his regiments, the 33d, captured but quickly relinquished a battery which ventured near a thicket in which it was lying.

Dr. Dabney does not notice this statement of Beauregard, but his account concurs with mine.

upon to express his opinion in a council of war, nor were the other subordinate generals; but he could not restrain the expression of his desire from his immediate companions, and it was in accordance with the policy which characterized his entire career.

McDowell's army was not only beaten—it was routed; and our losses had not impaired the efficiency of our troops. General Johnston has attempted to excuse himself in a communication published since the war, in which he says: "The substantial fruit of this victory was the preservation of the Confederacy. No more could have been hoped for. The pursuit of the enemy was not continued because our cavalry (a very small force) was driven back by the 'solid resistance' of the United States infantry. Its rear guard was an entire division, which had not been engaged, and was twelve or fifteen times more numerous than our two little bodies of cavalry. The infantry was not required to continue the pursuit, because it would have been harassing it to no purpose. It is well known that infantry, unencumbered by baggage trains, can easily escape pursuing cavalry."[*]

This apology is not in keeping with the usual candid good sense of General Johnston. The rear guard he speaks of was Miles' division, 10,000 strong, which had during the day held the ridge between Centreville and Blackburn's Ford, (Longstreet's position,) and which had withdrawn to the heights of Centreville to cover the retreat of McDowell. It there drew up in line of battle, only five miles from our right wing, and its "solid resistance" consisted in its firing at a handfull of cavalry which reconnoitered it. How can General Johnston say "solid resistance," when he confesses at the same time that he did not send his infantry to test it? He stated with equal disingenuousness to Mr. Swinton that "in our condition pursuit could not be thought of; for we were almost as much disorganized by our victory as the Federals by their defeat."[†] This is not true. Our army was in admirable condition and spirit to follow. On the morning of July 21st General Beauregard had 21,833 effective men and twenty-nine cannon, and 6,000 bayonets and twenty guns of Johnston's army had arrived.[‡] Two thousand infantry under Smith and Elzey had arrived during the fight, and we had, therefore, at the end of the day, 29,833 men, and forty-nine pieces of artillery on the field. Comparatively, a small proportion had been engaged. General Johnston

---

*Alfriend's Life of Jefferson Davis.
†Swinton: Army of the Potomac, p. 59.
‡Beauregard's Report: Reports of Manassas, p. 11.

says in his report: "The admirable character of our troops is incontestibly proved by the result of this battle; *especially when it is remembered* that little more than 6,000 men of the Army of the Shenandoah, with sixteen guns, and less than 2,000 of that of the Potomac, with six guns, for full five hours successfully resisted 35,000 United States troops, with a powerful artillery and a superior force of regular cavalry. Our forces engaged, gradually increasing during the remainder of the contest, amounted to but   at the close of the battle." The blank might be filled by 10,000; for the increase consisted in 2,000 under Smith and Elzey, and a few regiments of Beauregard's army, not exceeding 2,000 more. We had, therefore, (nearly) 20,000 fresh troops lying idle within five miles of this "solid resistance"—troops, too, who had not marched or been taxed by any arduous service, and had nothing to demoralize them. The Federal writers are of course prompt to adopt General Johnston's theory, as the demoralization imputed to our troops is complimentary to the fight their own had made, and palliates their demoralization afterwards. But the proof that we were not demoralized to any very considerable extent is almost as strong as the proof that they were. Says General McDowell in his report: "The retreat soon became a rout, and this presently degenerated into a panic." The extent of that panic has become a matter of world-wide notoriety. There can be no question as to the success of our army if it had pushed on; the only question is what was the proper course for our generals under the lights before them. That the Federal army had been terribly beaten was evident. One thousand four hundred and sixty prisoners remained in our hands, twenty-eight pieces of artillery, over five thousand muskets, and the field itself bore testimony of a rout. Under these circumstances, we should have at least pressed forward and tested the so-called "solidity" of that resistance, which consisted in firing a few guns at a reconnoitering body of cavalry. It was not and could not have been expected that a handfull of cavalry could break an infantry division, and no serious attack was made; but if our 20,000 fresh infantry and our fifty pieces of artillery had been hurled against it, who can doubt but that it would have been brushed away like a cobweb. No one could have blamed Johnston had he attacked the rear guard and found it impracticable to destroy it; but he is greatly to be blamed for making no effort. The apprehension that Patterson would soon join McDowell ought only to have accelerated Johnston to complete the destruction of the latter before his arrival. Even had he arrived the united force would not have exceeded 30,000 effectives, and no General of revolutionary spirit ought to have hesitated to attack them, weary and dispirited as they must have been, with 20,000 fresh men elated with victory.

The joy of the South over what was done at Manassas, dulled its criticism at the loss of the opportunity to do more; but a calm view of the question flash conviction upon the mind that Johnston and Beauregard were lacking in the insight that recognizes, and the boldness that improves a lucky moment. "Opportunity," it has been said "has hair in front; behind she is bald; if you catch her by the forelock, you may hold her; but if suffered to escape Jupiter himself cannot catch her again." Such is the moral of Manassas.

VIII

During the winter of 1861, Jackson was appointed a Major-General and sent to the Valley of Virginia, and there in the spring of 1862 he led his army through that series of marches and actions which are known as "The Valley Campaign," and in which he seemed, like the fabled Knight of Old Castile, to bear an enchanted lance which struck every enemy it aimed at, and struck only to conquer.

A mere summary of the facts of the Valley Campaign is the best tribute to the ability of its hero.

On the 9th of March, 1862, General J. E. Johnston fell back from Centreville where he had confronted General McClellan during the previous winter, and on the 11th inst. General Jackson fell back from Winchester before General Banks who was advancing with 35,000 men; and halted at Mount Jackson on the "Valley pike" between Winchester and Staunton, and forty miles from the former town. On the 21st of the month he learned that Banks had detached 15,000 men under General Sedgwick to join the army opposed to General Johnston in Eastern Virginia, and that the remainder, under General Shields, was moving up the pike against him. He instantly put his troops in motion. He marched 26 miles on the 22d inst., and 16 on the 23d, and that evening attacked Shields at Kernstown, a little hamlet three miles south of Winchester. Shields had 11,000 men

in action. Jackson had only 2,742 infantry, 18 pieces of cannon,
and 290 cavalry. He did not drive the enemy from the field, but he
accomplished his main object of recalling Sedgwick's column from
its movement against General Johnston, crippled the enemy severely,
taught him a wholesome dread of the audacity and vehemence of his
attacks. General Shields was left like Pyrrhus after Heraclea, to feel
that another such victory would destroy him. He claimed that our
sufferings were terrible, but added, with soldierly candor, " yet such
were their gallantry and high state of discipline that at no time
during the battle or pursuit did they give way to panic."* The
Southern people received the tidings of the battle with similar appreciation, and the Confederate Congress passed a resolution of thanks
to Jackson and his soldiers for their gallant services.

After the battle, Jackson retired to the vicinity of Harrisonburg,
and the two armies lay quiescent until the 1st of May, on which day
he received a reinforcement of General Ewell's division from the
army of General Johnston which swelled his force to about 15,000
men of all arms—and he now prepared to resume hostilities.

Jackson was now menaced from two points. Banks confronted
him from the north with 20,000 men, while Milroy, on the mountains west of Staunton, lay off on his left flank with 8,000 men, who
were opposed by the single brigade of General Edward Johnson.
Leaving Ewell to manage Banks, Jackson marched rapidly up the
Valley, passed through Staunton, united with Edward Johnson, and
on the 9th of May dispatched the result to Richmond :

" God blessed our arms with victory at McDowell yesterday."

Milroy retreated precipitously into West Virginia, and Jackson
returned with his flying light infantry to renew his attentions to
Banks. During the rest of May, he was continuously marching and
fighting. On the 23d he drove Banks through Front Royal, and
captured with little loss 700 prisoners and 2 cannon. On the 25th
he pursued him through Winchester. On the 28th he dispersed his
rear guard on the banks of the Potomac. On the 30th of May,
having retired to the vicinity of Winchester, he had reason to appre-
hend that Fremont, from the northwest was endeavoring, with a large
force, to gain his rear near Strasburg. Moving at noon that day, he
reached Strasburg the next, having marched the astonishing distance
of fifty miles in 40 hours, with an army encumbered by 1,500 wagons,
more than 50 artillery carriages, and 2,300 prisoners.

* Shields' Report.

Within twenty-two days he had marched over 350 miles, fought two battles and six combats; with only 12,000 men, had defeated two armies aggregating 30,000 men, had captured 3,000 prisoners, 1,000 stand of arms; had supplied his medical and ordnance trains, and fed and clothed his hungry and naked troops on captured stores; had lost only 68 killed, 329 wounded, and 3 missing, and had finally extricated himself and his spoils from a dangerous position.

None can doubt that men capable of such marches were as worthy of the soubriquet of "foot cavalry" as when at bay they deserved to be called "a stonewall:" and well might their general have told them, as Napoleon told the Army of Italy, that he had rather gain victories at the expense of their legs than their blood.

These are pregnant facts, though not exhibited in a critical arrangement. Cross Keys and Port Republic, the twin battles on the Shenandoah, remain to be recounted as the fit climax to terminate the Valley campaign, as the broad and solid but delicately wrought Corinthian capital crowns the stately marble column.

To appreciate them it is necessary to glance at the topographical features of the country adjacent, and the relation of Jackson's army to the Army of Northern Virginia which under Lee was guarding Richmond.

A glance at the map will show that the operations of all the armies in eastern Virginia at this time were embraced within a parallelogram of which the Potomac from Williamsport to Washington was the northern, and the Central Railroad between Staunton and Richmond the southern side; the Valley pike, a broad paved highway from Williamsport to Staunton, the western, and the Richmond and Fredericksburg Railroad and the Potomac river, uniting Richmond and Washington, the eastern side. Jackson, it will thus be seen, while guarding the Central Railroad by his position in the Valley, had so to manœuvre as to be able, in the event of a necessary retreat, to join his forces with the utmost rapidity with the main army of Lee at Richmond.

Turning to the immediate scene of operations, we find him on the evening of the 1st of June at Strasburg with about 15,000 men. Fremont was immediately in front of him with 20,000 followers,*

---

*The north and south forks of the Shenandoah unite at Front Royal, and the north fork crosses the Valley pike several times, but its course did not materially affect the campaign.

and Shields, with about 7,000, was at Front Royal, on his right flank, but separated from him by the north and south forks of the Shenandoah river. On that evening Jackson commenced a retreat up the Valley pike, followed by Fremont, while Shields continued to move on the eastern side of the south fork of the Shenandoah, which flows parallel to the main pike. Had Shields and Fremont combined at once, their overwhelming numbers would have indeed presented a terrible head to Jackson, but a stream swollen by spring rains was between them, their pontoons had been destroyed in a retreat shortly previous, and Jackson's manœuvres were all directed with a view of keeping them apart, and seizing any opportunity of taking advantage of their separation. Having succeeded in destroying the bridges on the south fork in the course of his retreat, we find him on the 6th of June as far up the Valley as Harrisonburg, closely pressed by Fremont; and on that day, while gallantly bringing up his rear guard, fell Ashby—that bright ideal of a soldier, in whose character were beautifully blended the romantic hues of chivalry with the solid virtues of a Southern patriot.* Even amidst the clash of arms the involuntary tear starts to the eye over his early grave:

"Brief, brave and glorious was his young career—
His mourners were two hosts, his friends and foes;
And fitly may the stranger lingering there
Pray for his gallant spirit's bright repose—
For he was Freedom's champion; one of those,
The few in number, who had not o'erstep't
The charter to chastise which she bestows
On such as wield her weapons. He had kept
The whitness of his soul, and thus men o'er him wept."

From Harrisonburg Jackson diverged eastward, and leaving Ewell with his division at "Cross Keys," a country cross roads nine miles distant, he moved five miles further on, and halted near the village of

*Ashby was interred in the graveyard at the University of Virginia, but his remains were removed after the war to his mother's home in Fauquier. In his report, Jackson thus alluded to his untimely end: "An official report is not an appropriate place for more than a passing notice of the distinguished dead; but the close relation which General Ashby bore to my command for most of the previous twelve months will justify me in saying that as a partizan officer I never knew his superior. His daring was proverbial; his powers of endurance almost incredible; his tone of character heroic, and his sagacity almost intuitive in divining the purposes and movements of the enemy."—*Reports of the Army of Northern Virginia, Vol. I, page 55.*

E

Port Republic, which nestles in the fork formed by the North and South rivers which there combine into the south branch of the Shenandoah. The South river is there fordable, but the North river could be crossed only by a bridge; and remaining on the north-west side of that stream, Jackson awaited the movements of Fremont in that direction, and guarded the bridge from the approach of Shields from the north-east. Early* on the morning of Sunday, the 8th day of June, Jackson, with a few attendants, crossed the North river into Port Republic, and while there the vanguard of Shields made its appearance, and rushing rapidly across the ford of South river, captured two of his staff, and placed a piece of artillery at the southern end of the bridge. Thus cut off from his soldiers and surrounded by his enemies, Jackson was in a perilous quandary. But his ingenious audacity saved him. Galloping up to the commander of the gun at the bridge he exclaimed in a tone of authority: "Who told you to place this gun here, sir? Remove it instantly to yonder hill." Presuming him to be of course a Federal officer of rank, the artillerist obeyed his order promptly, and Jackson bounded over the bridge to his camps. Quickly getting his men under arms he hurried back to the bridge, leading the thirty-seventh Virginia regiment, the first to hand, and directing its charge, it swept over the bridge, and, losing but two men from the enemy's fire, captured the gun, and cleared the village of the adventurous advance guard which a moment before held the army at its mercy. This little affair had scarcely transpired when Shield's army appeared in force on the eastern side of the south fork of the Shenandoah, and at 10 o'clock, A. M., firing in the direction of Cross Keys announced that Fremont had come in contact with Ewell. Jackson's situation was critical in the extreme. His army, in two divisions, his own and Ewell's, aggregated a little over 12,000 men, and two armies were now closing in upon him, and were within hearing of each other's guns. Crowning the hills on the north-east bank of the river at Port Republic with cannon, and making as great a show as his meagre forces could against Shields, he galloped at midday to Ewell's lines at Cross Keys and beheld him holding Fremont gallantly at bay. Returning quickly, he sent Ewell two brigades, Taylor's of Ewell's division, (which he had taken to strengthen him-

*This story is told in the Life of Jackson, by an Ex-Cadet, and in Doolady's also. It is not mentioned in Dr. Dabney's or in Cooke's, and this fact may throw some doubt on its authenticity. It has been generally circulated, however, and I have never heard it contradicted.

self early in the morning,) and Patton's, of his own, and with these additions the noble Ewell, who had already repulsed Fremont's attacks, advanced upon him, drove in his skirmish line, and keeping up a bold demonstration, intimidated him by an appearance of strength and desire for battle. Shields, bluffed during the day by Jackson's energetic preparations at Port Republic, had subsided into inactivity, and with matters in this attitude night closed.

Jackson had so far thwarted the peril that hung over him, but it was still imminent, and in all probability would burst upon him on the morrow. To retreat was to leave Fremont and Shields to unite and follow him. To stand still was to permit them to crush him by sheer weight of numbers. He solved the problem by resolving to be himself the assailant. Causing a foot bridge of wagons to be constructed during the night across the ford of the South river, he withdrew Ewell's division from Cross Keys, leaving only Patton's and Trimble's brigades to make a bold face before Fremont, and crossing the river early on the morning of the 9th, he attacked Shields with fury. The battle was hard fought, but he drove the Federals from the field and captured 450 prisoners and nine pieces of artillery. Sending his cavalry in pursuit of the beaten army, he withdrew Patton and Trimble from Fremont's front in the evening, destroyed the bridge over North river, and thus left Fremont to gnash his teeth in impotent rage while Shields fled in disaster.

Jackson now retired to Brown's Gap, a few miles distant, from which point he could easily retreat into the interior if he found it necessary, or return as assailant. Fremont remained a day or two at Port Republic when hearing how Shields had been used up, he also retreated hastily down the valley, leaving his sick, wounded, and hospitals behind him, and Jackson to prepare for his brilliant march to assist Lee at Richmond.

The campaign had much a deeper significance than appears from following its marches, and battles. The strokes of Jackson not only broke the limbs they fell upon, but shocked the whole system of hostile operations.

On the 25th of May when he drove Banks through Winchester, McDowell's corps numbering forty-one thousand men, and one hundred cannon had advanced eight miles south of Fredricksburg on its way to join McClellan, who was then investing Richmond. McClelland had thrown forward his right wing to Hanover Junction to meet him, and they were but fifteen miles apart. The very next day they were to combine and assail Johnston with resistless numbers. But just then the news of Jackson's advance was flashed to Washington, McDowell was instantly recalled, and 20,000 of his men were hurried off to the Shenandoah Valley to stay the terrible hand of Jackson.* The fairest and most reliable critic of the war observes "that without gaining a single tactical victory Jackson had yet achieved a great strategic victory, for by manœvering 15,000 men he had succeeded in neutralizing a force of 60,000 men."† When he struck McClellan at Richmond a month later, McDowell petrified by his name, laid motionless at Fredricksburg—afraid to uncover the front of Washington, and we may justly confirm the judgment of the same critic that "it is perhaps not too much to say he saved Richmond."

I once heard an officer ask General Ewell what he thought of Jackson's generalship in this campaign. He replied in his brusque impetuous manner : "Well sir when he commenced it, I thought him crazy, before he ended it, I thought him inspired." The campaign was not one of large numbers, but its manœuvers were so rapid, so bold, so energetic, and so delicately calculated that they could only have been executed by a master of the Art of War. Those who at its beginning thought its movements erratic, and called Jackson "crazy" soon found that there was a "method in his madness," like that of the Macedonian madman which brought order from chaos, and had its sequel in victory.

Jackson had carved his way to enduring fame and the "Valley

---

* For these facts see Swinton's Army of the Potomac p. 125-6. His comments are worth quoting "In vain General McClellan urged the real motion of the raid—to prevent reinforcements from reaching him. Deaf to all sounds of reason, the war-council at Washington, like the Dutch States-General, of whom Prince Eugene said that "always interfering they were always dying with fear" heard only the reverberations of the guns of the redoubtable Jackson. To head off Jackson, if possible to catch Jackson, seemed now the one important thing; and the result of the cogitations of the Washington strategists was the preparation of what the President called a "trap" for Jackson—a "trap" "for the wily fox who was master of every gap and gorge of the Valley !"

We have seen already what became of the trap.

† Mr. Swinton is as palpably mistaken in saying that Jackson had not gained a "single tactical victory" as General Johnston was (see ahead) in saying Jackson was not a great strategist. Port Republic and Cross-Keys beautifully combine the excellencies of tactical and strategic genius.

campaign" will be preserved in history as a model for the military
student to study, and a feat for mankind to admire.*

> "His schemes of war were sudden, unforseen—
> Inexplicable both to friend and foe;
> It seems as if some momentary spleen
> Inspired the project and compelled the blow,
> And most his fortune and success were seen—
> With means the most inadequate and low;
> Most master of himself and least encumbered,
> When overmatched, entangled and outnumbered."

IX

No general ever evinced a truer appreciation of the value of time
in military operations, and in no war has time ever been so valuable
an element as in that for Southern Independence. We fought against
time.   We had a limited quantity of ammunition; we had the mini-
mum quantity of food; we had only a certain number of men.
General Grant was glad to swap five men for one of Lee's; he could
wait six months for a victory.   An army or an hour lost with us was
lost forever—with the Federals spring-time brought reinforcements
and leisure. "I have observed," said Napoleon, "that it is the
quarters of hours that decide the fate of battles."   Jackson never
lost time!   He struck the enemy to-day—he did not wait for him to
rest and reconstruct to-morrow—he followed him and struck him
again while stunned, sore and exhausted.   The old fogies, and the
red-tape men of the army swore he was crazy when he was marching
to Romney after the Yankees in the winter of 1861, while the
Yankees themselves, and the rest of our own army were nestling so
cosily in winter quarters—but he was seasoning his oak in winter to
stand the storms of spring. The manner in which dulled stupidity
talked of him then and at the beginning of the Valley Campaign,
was very much in the strain of the old Hungarian officer who ridi-
culed Napoleon's strategy after he had beaten the Austrians out of
Italy.   "Things are going on as ill, and as irregularly as possible," said

---

* Dr. Dabney (p. 429) says "within forty days he had marched four hundred miles, fought four pitched battles—defeating four separate armies,
with numerous combats and skirmishes, sent to the rear three thousand
five-hundred prisoners, killed and wounded a still larger number of the
enemy, and defeated or neutralized forces three times as numerous as his
own."

the old Martinet. "The French have got a young general who knows nothing of the regular rules of war; he is sometimes in our front, sometimes on our flank, sometimes on the rear. There is no supporting such a gross violation of the rules."* And this, as Scott observes, somewhat resembles the charge that foreign tacticians have brought against the English that they gained victories by continuing, with their insular ignorance and obstinacy, to fight on long after the period when, if they had known the rules of war, they ought to have considered themselves as completely defeated. Jackson was like the young French general when he attacked; he was like the obstinate Englishmen when he stood at bay.

On the front, on the flank, on the rear of the Yankees—he seemed often to happen at the very point where they least expected to find him, and often to fly from point to point so fast that like a moving brand he made around them a circle of fire. His infantry was called by the army "Jackson's foot cavalry," and "the foot cavalrymen" jestingly declared that he was greater than Moses. "Moses," they said, "took forty years to lead the Israelites through the Wilderness with manna to feed them on ; old Jackson would have double-quicked through it on half rations in three days." A wag sent him a letter addressed, "Stone W. Jackson, Esqr., somewhere or somewhere else."

Prompt selection of the point to aim it, all the energies roused up to hit it, not an instant's hesitation as to striking, and striking again—we see in every action. After the battle of Manassas, while our other generals were talking about rations for the men, and about the "solid resistance" of one division of United States infantry at Centreville, Jackson was in favor of pushing on to Washington at once—only thirty miles off, knowing very well that there was plenty of rations there, and that the resistance of that infantry would not be less solid when Patterson's 18,000 had strengthened it, and when it had recovered from the dismay produced by a routed army fleeing through and all around it. He always followed up his victories in the Valley, for there was no superior officer there to prevent him. He was in favor of pursuing McClellan when he was cowering under his gunboats at Harrison's Landing. He was in favor of crushing Burnside when we had him under our heel on the banks of the Rappahannock. He attacked Hooker at Chancellorsville the instant our troops got into line of battle, and the last order which he ever gave on the field was "tell A. P. Hill to press right on."

* Scott's Napoleon I, p. 318.

We have heard some of our timid generals defended for not pushing the enemy, on the ground that they held back out of regard for their men. We have only to answer that they had false and narrow views of what was best for their men. If they had concentrated their forces, made and followed up a vigorous, well sustained attack, and pressed every advantage they might have lost more fearfully during any given half hour, but they would have saved the terrible waste of prolonged campaigns and decimating camp diseases, and the oft-repeated losses of minor battles, and would not only have gained a field, but garnered up the fruits of victory. The fact is, that the terrific system of war which hurls masses of men upon one point—mass after mass, and is so often condemned as brutal, is the most humane in the end, because the most effective. Napoleons, Cæsars, Jacksons are not the spend-thrifts, but the wise economists of human life; and those cautious and over-sensitive captains who are afraid to push the battle lest somebody be hurt, are more misers, "penny-wise and pound-foolish"—they guard their treasure like the unfaithful steward by burying it in the ground, and rendering it incapable of producing good either to themselves or others.

The general should have tender feelings, but he should have a will capable of restraining them when to indulge them is ruin. "O that I had time to weep" exclaims Napoleon in a note to a mother, after battle announcing that her son was slain, but it would have been not less a crime than a weakness for him to have paused to weep over one mother's son when thousands of others stood in peril, and depended on him to shield them.

Those military men who claim exoneration for failure on account of tender feelings, are on a par with surgeons who faint at the sight of blood. They have mistaken their calling, and only reveal their weak nerves and their weak heads. They play the hero like Bottom played the lion in Pyramus and Thisbe promising to modulate his voice in order not to frighten the ladies: "1 will roar you gently as any sucking dove; I will roar you gently an'twere any nightingale." Doves and nightingales are excellent things in their way; but when we send for lions we prefer that they should bring their roar and their claws with them, and that they should not indulge themselves on the battle field in cooing and billing. Some of our military lions succeeded admirably in not frightening the ladies—or anybody else.

Others of our generals apologized for not pursuing after battle on account of a lack of wagons, and bridges, and rations. That was one of the excuses made after the first battle of Manassas. Jackson forded rivers, or improvised bridges, and did without wagons and rations until he caught the enemy and captured them. "What creates difficulty," said Napoleon, "in the profession of the land commander is the necessity of feeding so many men and animals. If he allows himself to be guided by the commissaries he will never stir, and all his expeditions will fail." Whenever the majority of the generals in the late war started on an expedition a commissary pulled them back by the coat tail. When Jackson started he kicked the commissary out of the way and went without him.

His own cooks were like those of Alexander, a march before day to dress his dinner, a light dinner to prepare his supper—and as for supper, he took that next day; and his troops fared like him. Victory, however, was generally his commissary, and kept him well supplied from the enemy's camps.

After Jackson had taken Harper's Ferry, he conversed with a group of captive officers. "Has McClellan a drove of cattle with him?" he asked. "Yes," was the reply—"a large one." "Well," said the General, "I can whip any army that travels with a drove of cattle"—alluding both to the sluggishness it necessitated on their part, and to the keen appetites of his men. General Banks was oftener spoken of as the commissary general of Jackson than as his adversary in the field. His trains had filled our haversacks so often that whenever the head of the column turned down the Valley, the jest ran along the lines: "Lee is out of rations again, and Jackson is detailed to call on the commissary general."

X

Plain common sense, moral courage, and decision of character, "the will to do, the soul to dare," were the germs of all Jackson's great deeds. His will was never surpassed. As a mere pulp of paper can be driven through oaken plank when a powerful combustible is exploded behind it, so may an ordinary mind penetrate the most unyielding obstacles when propelled by a powerful determination; while in an infants hand the most terrible projectile becomes only a dangerous toy.

An English essayist, Foster, tells us of a father who had two sons, both of whom had been condemned to die for some capital crime. The king of their country in pity for the old man sent him word that one of his sons should be spared, and that he must make the selection within a certain hour. The old man first thought of the talents of one son, and then of the graces and affection of the other, preferring each as his virtues arose before his mind, but unable to decide between them; and thus in an agony of suspense and hesitation, the hour went by and he was roused from deliberation by the announcement that the law had been enforced, and both were dead. We could recall several instances during the late war, in which commanding generals acted with similar weakness. When they were approached by columns in different directions, instead of instantly striking one, they stood in painful trepidation between the two—now calculating the chances of defeating one, now reconnoitering and faintly skirmishing with the other. In a short time the two united, and they were then either beaten by largely superior numbers, or forced to make a "masterly retreat" under hot pressure, and write an elaborate official report to show that they had abandoned the field in strict accordance with the art of war. Thus it is with the indecisive man. He deliberates when the time for deliberation is past, and when any decisive action is better than none. The opportunity is gone forever, and no expenditure of treasure or blood, and no resource of genius can restore it. In such emergencies Jackson's mind quickly formed a plan, and roused up all its energies for its execution—and then came into play that sublime courage which like Cæsar's, was twin-born with danger, and taught danger that it was more dangerous than he.

Mere physical courage is a common quality. The gentleman is brave from instinct, and the hireling from fear of his officer. In the South especially, personal daring is so general a characteristic, that the lack of it was exceptional, and every field of the late war was illustrated by astonishing feats of valor which did not attract the attention they deserved, because it was impossible to make discriminations and they were really "too numerous to mention." And in many cases if any fault could be found with our troops, it was that fearlessness degenerated into recklessness, and the hot-blooded Southerner became

> "More brave than firm, and more inclined to dare
> And die at once—than wrestle with despair."

But the courage which does not shrink from responsibility, and

F

remains self-poised and imperturbable under sudden dangers is amongst all peoples a rare personal characteristic.

"As to moral courage," said Napoleon, "I have rarely met with the two o'clock in the morning kind. I mean unprepared courage, that which is necessary to an unexpected occasion, and which in spite of unforeseen events leaves full freedom of judgment and decision." That two o'clock in the morning courage existed in Jackson to perfection. He never lost the "full freedom of judgment and decision,"[*] but himself declared that "he was conscious of a more perfect command of all his faculties when under fire than at any other time," and his whole career is filled with striking illustrations of that self-possession which calmly met the most startling and perilous emergencies, and disposed of them with easy and decisive promptitude. It shone at Manassas, at Kernstown, at Fort Republic—it shone everywhere. When others lost faith he stood firm in a faith that removed mountains; when lines were broken, plans disorganized, resources of skill were exhausted, and the fugitives' wild cry, "all is lost," arose over a mangled and bleeding field—still with lip firm, with eye fixed, he clung to his post with the tenacity of destiny until reänimated by his example cowards became men, men became heroes, and heroes seemed to tower into demigods—and victory was plucked from the gulf of despair.

In point of talent Jackson was surpassed by many of the generals who fought with and against him. He was inferior to Johnston in intellectual power and in ability for laying complicated and far-reaching schemes. His mind was not so broad and capacious as Lee's. He was not so scientific as Beauregard, or so variously accomplished as McClellan. He had not the mental vigor or scope of Early. But he more happily combined than any the cool audacity, the imperturbable resolution, and the wonderful earnestness which struck a terror into his enemy's hearts that half conquered them before battle, and an enthusiasm into his soldiers which made them irresistible. This balance of common sense and courage is worth all other qualities whatsoever. Napoleon, discoursing on the requisites of a military commander, remarks: "We rarely find combined together all the qualities requisite to constitute a great general. The object most desirable is that a man's judgment should be in equilibrium with his physical character or courage. This is what we may call

---

[*] Dabney, p. 52.

being squared both by base and perpendicular. If courage be in the ascendency, a general will rashly undertake that which he cannot execute; on the contrary, if his character or courage be inferior to his judgment he will not venture to carry any measure into effect. The sole merit of the Viceroy Eugene consisted in this equilibrum. This, however, was sufficient to render him a very distinguished man." We readily recognize this equilibrium in Jackson. He retreated from Kernstown. He advanced to McDowell. He had the precaution to retire from Winchester, and the audacity to assail at Cross Keys and Manassas. He cautiously vacated Pope's front at Cedar Mountain, and with boldness bordering on rashness he hung upon his rear at Manassas, and charged Hooker in reverse at Chancellorsville. His actions were the exemplication of the inscription on the gates of the ancient city: "Be bold! Be evermore bold! *Be not too bold!*"

Lord Macaulay expressed in different language the same idea expressed by Napoleon: "An unlearned person," he says, "would be inclined to suspect that the military art is no very profound mystery; that its principles are principles of plain good sense; and that a quick eye, a cool head, and a stout heart do more to make a General than all the diagrams of Jomini."* So we have the greatest of generals and the best of critics on a common platform. The truth is, the faculty for commanding men, and for leading enterprises "of great pith and moment" is barely akin to those brilliant talents which shine in devising theories for others to execute, or executing those which have been devised for them. Many a learned and eloquent barrister who can wring tears and verdicts from jurymen, becomes a worthless pedagogue when elevated to the responsibility of the bench. Many an ingenious diplomatist who exposes the folly of cabinets and parliaments, becomes irresolute and impracticable when made prime minister and told to inaugurate a policy of his own. And many a highly educated and intelligent officer, who would storm a fort gallantly, and who has all the theories of tactics, strategy, fortification, and engineering at his fingers' ends, sinks into confusion and helplessness when the destinies of an army are placed in his keeping and the boom of cannon tells him that the hour of trial is at hand.

The man of knowledge and the man of action are of an entirely different mould. Knowledge is invaluable in directing action, but

---

*Article on Hampden: Essays, p. 160.

common sense availing itself of the knowledge of others is an excellent substitute; while on the other hand knowledge, unless set on fire by action, is nothing more than so much powder stored away in a magazine. The difference between the learned plodder and the gifted man of action was admirably illustrated by John Randolph, of Roanoke, in the fable of the huntsman and the caterpillar, which has a savor of real Æsopian salt. A caterpillar comes to a fence; he crawls to the bottom of the ditch and over the fence—some one of his hundred feet always in contact with the object upon which he moves. A gallant horseman, at a flying leap, clears both ditch and fence. "Stop," says the caterpillar, "you are too flighty—you want connection and continuity; it took me an hour to get over; you can't be as sure as I am, who have never quitted the subject, that you have overcome the difficulty and are fairly over the fence." "Thou miserable reptile," replies the huntsman, "if like you I crawled over the earth slowly and painfully, should I ever catch a fox or be anything more than a wretched caterpillar?" The learned caterpillars of the war when they approached an obstacle generally wasted two or three days in reconnoitering it, and their skirmishers, like so many hundred feet, felt the position with the utmost caution. After the enemy had entirely recovered from surprise and had fully fortified and prepared for them, they crawled up to the attack with elaborate dullness, and after getting a good threshing made a "masterly retreat." They never caught a federal fox, and despite their excellent official reports were never anything but wretched caterpillars. Jackson comes with his army like a gallant huntsman on a well-bred hunter, and the ear of the startled picket had scarcely caught the clatter of a hoof, or the yelp of the hound, ere he and his pack of hungry, ragged, cheering rebels was upon them. (The enemy began to fear him as the fox the bloodhound.) In his very name they scented a portent of danger and heard a presage of victory. The French nurses, we are told, frightened their children with stories of "Marlbrook," and the Orientals, when their horses started, imagined that they saw the shadow of Richard Cœur de Leon crossing their path.* The Yankees, when they heard the ominous words: "Jackson is moving," felt the dread instinct of a mysterious danger, which only warned with fatal blows, and hied away to their fortifications.

---

*Alison's Marlborough.

It cannot with any propriety be said that "luck" was the cause of Jackson's successes. They were not the fruits of a single victory, or of one campaign, or of favorable circumstances; but of vigorous campaigns following in swift succession and won through desperate battles, terrible obstacles, and a wide variety of hazardous adventures. The true test of a general, Napoleon declared, was not found in his escaping from difficulties and disasters, but in his coping boldly with and proving superior to them. Jackson was often environed with difficulties apparently insuperable and confronted with disaster. He invariably cut through difficulties, and changed disaster with the alchemy of genius into victory. His famous daring flank movements were never repeated, and the "luck" of striking the enemy in the rear and beating him with little loss, never afterward attended us—for the cause of that luck had departed.

You might as well say that luck produced the battle pictures of Horace Vernet as that it won Jackson's victories. Without brush and paint—without men and arms—the artist and the soldier could have done nothing. But many have had brush and paint—many have had more men and more arms—but none have brought forth from them such pictures, such victories.

One of his own soldiers threw into rough verse, a sketch of Jackson's way :*

> Come stack arms, men ; pile on the rails ;
>   Stir up the camp fires bright ;
> No matter if the canteen fails,
>   We'll make a roaring night.
> Here Shenandoah brawls along,
> There lofty Blue Ridge echoes strong
> To swell the Brigade's roaring song,
>   Of Stonewall Jackson's way !
>
> We see him now—the old slouched hat,
>   Cocked o'er his eye askew ;
> The shrewd dry smile, the speech so pat,
>   So calm, so blunt, so true.
> The "Blue-Light Elder" knows them well :
> Says he "that's Banks—he's fond of shell,
> Lord save his soul ! we'll give him——" well
>   That's Stonewall Jackson's way !

---

*This lyric came from an unknown lyre. "Des Rivierres" is the name appended in print, but who that is we have no idea.

Silence! ground arms! Kneel all! caps off!
    Old Blue Light's going to pray;
Strangle the fool that dares to scoff!
    Attention! it's his way!
Appealing from his native sod
In forma pauperis to God,
"Lay bare thine arm,—stretch forth thy rod,
    Amen!" That's Stonewall Jackson's way!

He's in the saddle now! fall in,
    Steady the whole Brigade,
Hill's at the Ford cut off! we'll win
    His way out, ball and blade.
What matter if our shoes are worn?
What matter if our feet are torn?
Quick step! we're with him before morn!
    That's Stonewall Jackson's way!

The sun's bright lances rout the mists
    Of morning—and by George!
There's Longstreet struggling in the lists
    Hemmed in an ugly gorge.
Pope and his columns whipped before—
"Bayonets and grape"—hear Stonewall roar;
"Charge Stuart! pay off Ashby's score!
    That's Stonewall Jackson's way!

Ah! maiden, wait and watch and yearn
    For news of Stonewall's band;
Ah! widow, read with eyes that burn,
    That ring upon thy hand.
Ah! wife sew on, pray on, hope on,
Thy life shall not be all forlorn;
The foe had better ne'er been born,
    Than get in Stonewall's way!

XI

General Joseph E. Johnston is said to have expressed the opinion that General Jackson was not a great strategist. General Johnston, we believe, was the most profound military man of the war—a man of cool, comprehensive and penetrating sagacity, but his opinion on this point is rebutted by the plain record of facts. The Valley campaign, and Richmond, and Manassas, and Chancellorsville rebuke it.

General Johnston, with talents of a superior order, was yet not so well fitted to lead such a forlorn hope as the Southern Revolution as General Jackson was. He was not so practical, so energetic, so daring. The Revolution depended upon audacious advances, not upon masterly retreats, and as soon as the retrogade system was adopted the days of the Confederacy were numbered. General Johnston's campaign in Georgia against Sherman was a master piece of military workmanship, and the spectacle of the hot-headed Minucius Hood, throwing away the rare opportunity that the skill of our Fabius had won, is the saddest of the war. But the Fabian policy, although skillfully carried out as it was by Johnston, was the wrong policy. The times did not call for Fabius—they wanted Scipio. We are proud of General Johnston's skill, but it was not the peculiar kind of skill that suited the obstacles we had to contend against. Jackson's was.

The Fabian policy was the judicious one for Washington and his generals during the Revolutionary War, because they made rivers, swamps, wildernesses, starvation and disease their allies. It was fatal to us because iron-clads, railroads, pontoon bridges, hospitals, telegraphs, with Germany, Ireland, and a united North, followed us, and we had nothing but naked patriotism to oppose them.

XII

The kindly relations of confidence, and friendship which existed between Jackson and Lee throw a genial light over the glory of both. Jackson said of his chief "Lee is a phenomenon, I would follow him blindfold." Lee said of him when wounded "Jackson has lost his left arm. I have lost my right arm;" and wrote to him with magnanimous sympathy: "could I have dictated events I should have chosen for the good of the country to have been disabled in your stead." "Far better for the Confederacy," exclaimed Jackson when he read the note, "that ten Jacksons should have fallen than one Lee." Criticism can only stand with uncovered head in the presence of such men—but criticism should be just in opinion, as well as generous in emotion. Comparing Jackson, and Lee the contrast is so striking that the comparison is difficult. For several reasons, however, we believe that Jackson was better suited to lead the armies of the revolution than Lee.

"Everywhere" says a brilliant historian of England "there is a class of men who cling with fondness to whatever is ancient, and who, even when convinced by overpowering reasons that innovation would be beneficial, consent to it with many misgivings, and forebodings. We find also another class of men sanguine in hope, bold in speculation, always pressing forward, quick to discern the imperfections of whatever exists, disposed to think lightly of the risks and inconveniences that attend improvements, and disposed to give every change credit for being an improvement."* Each class has its great representatives, and in war we find the one slow, methodical and cautious, and its glories are those of stubborn defence. The other never inactive pushes boldly forward, stakes all upon a well considered venture, and meets with decisive victory, or annihilation. Of one class Lee is a type, of the other Jackson—and Jackson's was the type we needed. Jackson was ambitious—Lee was not. Jackson sprung from poverty and obscurity, had to hew his way upward. Lee the scion of an influential, and aristocratic house which traced its lineage to the Norman conquest, the favorite subordinate of General Scott, the commander-in-chief of the United States Army, and his prospective successor, had nothing to gain from a disruption of the Union, but everything to lose. All of Lee's associations with the Government and the people were calculated to give a national and conservative tone to his character; the influences operating upon Jackson made him sectional and revolutionary. Lee's home was in full sight of the dome of the National Capitol, and he was admired and loved by all classes of the Capital city. He was besides on cordial terms of friendship with all the prominent officers of the army from the North, and felt a pang at the idea of severing his connection with a service which was endeared by the most sacred associations. When Virginia seceded there was a struggle in his bosom. He was opposed to the idea of a Southern Confederacy, and above all he was opposed to the peculiar institution which was to become its corner stone.† While thus wavering he was waited upon by a member of Mr. Lincoln's cabinet and tendered command of the United States Army.‡ The glittering bribe could not swerve the

---

* Macaulay, Vol. I. p. 93.

† "I have always been in favor of emancipation."—*Lee's testimony before Congressional Committee.*" McCabe's Life of Lee, p. 701.

‡ Hon. Montgomery Blair has so stated since the war in a published letter. See also McCabe, page 29.

pure soul of Robert Lee from its duty. A sentiment of honor bound him to his native State, and he determined to side with her, convinced though he was that her course was unwise, and held back as he was by his devotion to the Union. To his sister he wrote: "With all my devotion to the Union, and the feeling of loyalty and duty of an American citizen, I have not been able to make up my mind to raise my hand against my relatives, my children, my home. I have, therefore, resigned my commission in the army, and save in defence of my native State, with the sincere hope that my poor services may never be needed, I hope I may never be called upon to draw my sword."*

Locke has observed that there is no better proof of a man's greatness than his earnest efforts to carry out views which he originally opposed. It is a proof of Lee's greatness, and to his undying glory, that he promptly espoused the cause of his people when the issue was made up, and fought for it with unsurpassed heroism. But in criticising his campaigns we should not fail to estimate the effect of his political opinions upon his military character. Lee fought for a cause which he adopted with reluctance, and then not for its own sake, but simply from a technical view of its abstract right, and a warm-hearted sympathy with its people. This fact dampened his ardor and his hopes, and clouded his mind with misgivings and forebodings of an evil end. Heroically and magnificently as he fought, he did not fight with that confidence, that go-ahead-ativeness, that audacity, that fiery enthusiasm, which would have marked his course had his full faith fought with him.

Jackson, for a decade before the war, had mingled freely with and imbibed the sentiments of the people. He fully believed in the Southern Confederacy and in slavery, and he fought for both with the unshaken conviction that they were destined to endure, and that he was raised up to defend them.

Whether we are correct or not in conjecturing the causes of the difference in the military ideas and conduct of the two generals, certain it is that the difference existed. All the daring and brilliant strokes of the Army of Northern Virginia, after Lee assumed command of it, which were successful, were planned or executed by Jackson. In glancing at its battles we almost invariably behold Jackson at the crisis falling upon the enemy by a startling flank attack, and striking the fatal blow. It was his rapid march, his sud-

*McCabe, p. 31.

G

den apparition, and his sharp thrusts that turned McClellan from Richmond. It was Lee who checked pursuit at the river. It was Jackson who first beheld the "back of John Pope" at Cedar Run, and who by his adroit manoeuvres at Manasses held that redoubtable chieftain in check until Lee came up, and the two gave him a quietus together. To Jackson mainly is due the credit of capturing at Harper's Ferry 13,000 men and 73 pieces of cannon on the 15th of September, 1862, while on the day before Lee himself, at Boonsboro, having been tardy in bringing up Longstreet's division, received a rough handling from McClellan. They share jointly in the glories of Sharpsburg, but the only results of the Maryland campaign which redounded to our permanent benefit were those achieved by Jackson.

At Fredericksburg we behold a brilliant opportunity for crushing Burnside thrown away by Lee's over-caution. It is not doubted by either Federals or Confederates that had Lee pushed forward while Burnside's troops were crouching under the banks of the Rappahannock, he would have captured or destroyed them—Jackson was in favor of the effort at the time. It was Jackson, finally, who outdone Hooker at Chancellorsville, and it is a significant fact *that that was the last occasion on which the Army of Northern Virginia drove the Army of the Potomac beyond cannon range of the contest.*

At Gettysburg, three months afterwards, Lee stopped on the first day at the very moment of victory. On the second day he was beaten in detail in consequence of a disjointed and ill-regulated attack. On the third day the blunders of the second were fatally repeated. Many a soldier exclaimed, as he saw the opportunities of Gettysburg wasted, "oh for an hour of Jackson."

There was no fault to be found with the men. The Army was at the acme of its morale and physique at Gettysburg. It fought as well after its defeats as its victories, and as well after Jackson's death as before, but "it was noticed," as Mr. Swinton has observed "that Lee ventured upon no strokes of audacity after Jackson had passed away." *

The same author has expressed the opinion that "Jackson was essentially an executive officer, and though incomparable in that sphere, he was destitute of that power of planning and combination, and of that calm broad military intellect which distinguished General Lee."† But Jackson won his series of brilliant victories in the Valley

---

not as an executive officer, but as a general commanding with sole responsibility, and with no dependence on the counsel or direction of others. Jackson seemed more independent of Lee than Lee of him. His movements were generally of his own suggestion, and of that character whose chief merit consists in execution. Perhaps Lee's intellect was broader but it was not so keen. Against the mail-clad North the broad sword of Lee struck noble blows, but they could not cleave it. The rapier-like blade of Jackson penetrated the greaves and gave terrible wounds at every thrust.

Lee's ablest and most effective campaign was that against Grant from the Rappahannock to the James. The figures which attest Lee's excellent generalship, and Grant's bloody stolidity are startling. The armies met May 5th, 1864.* Grant had 125,000 effective men besides his reserve. Lee had 52,000. Grant's reinforcements up to June 3d, numbered 97,000; Lee's 18,000. Grant's total 222,000—Lee's total 70,000. Official returns show that up to 10th of June Lee had put 117,000 of Grant's men hors du combat, and lost but 19,000 of his own. "It will be seen that Grant's total force, including reinforcements, was 152,000, and his loss 9,800 in excess of Lee's, or that, with a force outnumbering his opponents three to one, Grant, the bungler, lost every other man in his army, while Lee lost but two out of every nine; or, that Grant lost just 6,000 men, more than one and a-half times Lee's entire army. That Grant succeeded is true but a general would have accomplished the same result with less means, and less loss." Such is the commentary of a Northern editor. It was derided when the South said that one of her soldiers was equal when defending his fireside to five of his enemies. Grant acknowledged it in his theory of the war, and proved it in his practice. On this campaign alone Lee's fame finds an imperishable foundation. It elevates him to the foremost rank of military men with Turenne, Eugene, Marlborough, and Wellington. No officer's abilities were ever more mathematically demonstrated than Lee's.

Adam Smith said "it is a characteristic almost peculiar to the great Duke of Marlborough that ten years of such uninterrupted, and splendid successes, as scarce any other general could boast of, never betrayed him into a single rash action, scarce into a single rash word or expression." Lee possessed the same temperate coolness, and self command as Marlborough without his weaknesses, or his

---

* This calculation is taken from the N. Y. World—June 9th, 1868.

vices. During four years of unremitting battle he stood calm, resolute, and imperturbable never betrayed by his varying fortunes into a single rash action, or uttering a rash expression. His enemies respected him scarce less than his friends, and it was equally honorable to him, and to the federal troops, that when a body of federal infantry passing down a street in Richmond after the surrender, caught a glimpse of his form, through a neighboring window, they raised their hats and gave him a splendid cheer.

Take him all in all he is greater as a man, but we think, not greater as a general, than Jackson.

The striking contrast between the universal popularity of Lee and Jackson, and the unpopularity of Jefferson Davis is explained by the fact that the former were simply soldiers—the latter a politician.

The North unanimously, and the South partially, referred the responsibility of the war to Mr. Davis. They knew that Lee and Jackson had no hand in bringing it about. Lee and Jackson had no associates in the North but friends. Davis, as the representative of Southern ideas and measures, had been thrown into fierce collision with Northern men from every State north of Mason's and Dixon's line. Lee parted from his old comrades in the army with tears in his eyes. Davis parted from his opponents in the Senate with indignation flashing in his. Davis was regarded by the North as erupting the Union and seeking to establish a new confederacy to gratify his personal ambition. Lee and Jackson were regarded as simply defending their people from a sentiment of duty.

These opinions must perish with the passions that engendered them, and the day will come when all classes will yield a hearty admiration to the great abilities and the unblemished character of Jefferson Davis. The hot lava of fanatical passion which would now destroy him, will when cool be wrought into images to his honor.

XIII

Our cause suffered incalculable injury from a radical source of evil for which the Confederate Congress was responsible mainly, and Davis, Lee, Jackson, and our other leaders secondarily; that is, the miserable unmilitary and unreasonable system of promotion in the Confederate Army which filled its high places with ignorant and incompetent officers. The officers of the regiments were originally elected—the privates choosing company officers, and the company officers choosing field officers. The vacancies constantly occurring were filled by regular gradation. Iago, in the Army of Northern Virginia, would have been delighted to see preferment go

> "by old gradation, where each second
> Stood heir to the first,"

though he would have seen many a "fellow" honored with stars and bars and wreaths,

> "Who never set a squadron in the field
> Nor the division of a battle knew
> More than a spinster."

In short, the men from personal favoritism chose the lieutenants and captains, and the enemy's bullets made the majors, colonels, and generals. A major, for instance, was killed. According to law the senior captain succeeded him, unless proved to be incompetent. However gifted, however well educated, however striking the military abilities or deserving the exploits of the second captain, he found an insurmountable obstacle to advancement in the person of his superior in rank. That technical superior might be ever so inferior in every essential, he still had the right to demand promotion. There was, therefore, no incentive to the laudable and generous aspirations of the subordinate officers. If they could manage to absent themselves from their regiments until their seniors were killed they were sure of promotion. If they performed prodigies of valor they could get it no sooner. Thus selfishness and mediocrity were starred and wreathed while patriotism and heroism bled and died in silence.

"*Quels sont les braves?*" Napoleon used to ask when he rode amongst his thinned ranks after a battle. When pointed out they were decorated with honors and advanced to high rank. No general of the South ever asked for the braves after a battle. They were left if wounded to lie unnoticed in hospitals; if unscathed, to fight on with every prospect of wounds and death, but without prospect of any reward save that of an approving conscience.

It is discreditable to the Confederate Government that it adopted such a system, and Lee, Jackson, and our other prominent generals, are to be blamed for tolerating it. True, these officers had no arbitrary power to remove the impediment, but they ought to have entered a daily protest against it, and persisted with all their energies in denouncing it. It was a deadly cancer in our military system, and proved fatal.

The Yankees did better. Like the French, they instantly degraded incompetence and rewarded merit. The consequence was that their officers were daily improving as a class, and ours depreciating. At the end of the war the best military talent of the North led its armies, and the best military talent of the South was still latent. Republican sensibilities were shocked during the Crimean war by the despicable regulation of the British service which forbade Lord Raglan to mention in an official report a non-commissioned officer who had saved his army. Common sense was as much shocked by the inability of the Confederate President to promote a private or sergeant to a captaincy because of the claims of a first lieutenant.

As dearly as we love, as truly as we honor Lee, and Jackson, and Davis, and Early, and Stuart, and their illustrious peers, far more warmly does the heart yearn, far more reverentially does the head bow to the devoted people whom they represented—the heroic army they led. History has heroes that stand on a level with our leaders —it has never had an army or a people that stand on so high a plane as our army and our people. It is impossible to separate them. Upon our battle fields we saw only the lessons of our firesides in action. As were the mothers, and sisters, and wives in the interior, so were the sons, brothers, and fathers in the front. The people were for the time absorbed in the army, and every true citizen of the South can justly share in the glory of the tribute thus spoken by one who fought against them: "Nor can there fail," says Mr. Swinton in his history; "Nor can there fail to arise the image of that other army that was the adversary of the Army of the Potomac—and which who can ever forget that once looked upon it? That array of 'tattered uniforms and bright muskets'—that body of incomparable infantry, the Army of Northern Virginia, which for four years carried the revolt upon its bayonets, opposing a constant front to the mighty concentration of power brought against it; which, receiving terrible blows, did not fail to give the like; and which, vital in all its parts, died only with its annihilation."*

---

*Swinton, p. 16.

XIV

Dr. Dabney in his work, repudiates the comparison of Jackson to Cromwell, but asserts that Jackson had all of Cromwell's genius "both military and civic;" * but it seems to us that the Doctor has at once over-estimated Jackson, and under-rated the great Puritan leader. Jackson was his equal—even his superior as a general, but whether or not he possessed comparable talents as a statesman must remain a matter of pure speculation.

Cromwell's abilities as a statesman were tested and proved by his course as a legislator, and as a ruler. Jackson's were never called into play,—and although, as his biographer shows, he expressed very sensible opinions on public affairs, there is not the slightest evidence that he had the genius which controls senates, and exercises a guiding influence on the complicated affairs of state. In point of intellect Jackson was far inferior to Cromwell. The letters, the speeches, and public acts of Cromwell reveal a deep knowledge of human nature, an administrative sagacity, and a high degree of versatility. Jackson has left us no speeeches,† and the letters from which Dr. Dabney has profusely quoted so far from shewing extensive information or profound observation are rather dull than otherwise, and would never be read but for the "shadow of a great name" that protects them.

A man of Jackson's earnestness is apt to succeed in any enterprise but there are no indications that he had peculiar fitness for the negotiations of diplomacy, the deliberations of cabinets, or the contests of the forum. The battle-field was his arena—he is not identified with any great idea of the South, but her genius for war found in him its best representative. The friends who make the assertion that he was intellectually great, do him injustice, and only lead to the disappointment of those who search his history for the verification.

There was nothing in his conversation, nothing in his writings, nothing in his deeds that unmistakeably indicate a comprehensive, or versatile mind; nor have those who were associated with him before or during the war, except in a few cases, held such an opinion; and the enlightened views of friends, and associates are fair criterions of character. These who lavish such compliments upon General Jackson do not appreciate the true elements of his heroic nature, and the true causes of his wonderful achievements.

* p. 13.

† A brief speech of Jackson to his troops is excepted. It is striking as a soldier's—nothing more.

XV

A comparison of Jackson to Napoleon, in point of genius, is utterly preposterous. Like Napoleon, Jackson was "a man of stone and iron, capable of sitting on horseback sixteen or seventeen hours, of going many days together without rest or food, except by snatches, and with speed and spring of a tiger in action ;"* but there the likeness ends. Napoleon was a universal man. Circumstances only determined whether he should be the greatest orator, poet, philosopher, law-giver, or scientific man of his age. He was so bountifully endowed by nature that he did become the leader of men in almost every department of learning and science. The grandest ideas of the grandest men of all times met together in his brain. The very glance of his eye consumed opposition like fire, and there "were words in him like Austerlitz battles." His profound calculations embraced continents—his minute observation descended to the spoke of a cannon wheel, and the buckle of a harness. Time, distance, mountains, seas, seasons, shrunk, expanded and changed at his dictation. The hemisphere adjusted itself to his notions. There was no genius like this in Jackson. Plain, silent, hard-working, brave and active, he succeeded not by extending his mind to embrace all elements, but by contracting it and keeping it steadily bent upon the study of war.

"Wellington," said Madame de Stael, "has not two ideas off the battlefield." There is a grain of truth in the remark. It was on the battle-field that great ideas sprung up in Jackson's brain—off of it he had none that would have made him memorable.

Morally Jackson towers as high above Napoleon as Napoleon towers intellectually above him. "I must dazzle and astonish," was the idea that lived and moved and had its being in Napoleon. "*Dieu et mon droit*" was incarnated in Jackson. Essentially selfish, Napoleon cared not what hearts were broken, what blood was spilled, provided the triumphal column held his image on its summit. Subordinating himself in all things to duty, Jackson had a heart for any fate, provided it were soothed by a still and quiet conscience. "As false as a bulletin" became a proverb in Napoleon's time—he became a text for the father of his to preach from—his bulletins had but one object, the glorification of self.

Read Jackson's dispatches—they are models of simplicity and

---

* Emerson's Representative Men, p. 226.

truth. When he is not informed as to facts, he is silent. Here are two:

> "VALLEY DISTRICT, *May 9, '62,*
> *via* STAUNTON, *May 10th.*

To GENERAL S. COOPER.

God blessed our arms with victory at McDowell yesterday.

> T. J. JACKSON, *Major-General.*"

> "PORT REPUBLIC, *June 9th,*
> *via* STAUNTON, *June 10th, 1862.*

To S. COOPER, *Adjutant-General.*

Through God's blessing, the enemy, near Port Republic, was this day routed with the loss of six pieces of his artillery.

> T. J. JACKSON, *Major-General.*"

This is his style—the usual exordium of acknowledgement to God—and then laconic statement of fact, in which no egotism intrudes.

The simplicity observable in his dispatches is observable in all his manners and actions. A writer from the army during the war very justly said, "General Jackson's head-quarters are often under a tree, and his couch is in a fence corner; his equipment is little more than a frying-pan and a blanket. He sees personally to the execution of his own orders. The activity of a perpetual 'forward' seems to pervade his army; they never get out of ammunition; they never lose baggage or stores; whether drawn from the government or captured from the enemy, no matter, they are always ready to move at the right time."*

XVI

We approach the last scene in the drama of Jackson's career.

The Army of Northern Virginia spent the winter of 1862–'63 on the banks of the Rappahannock, near Fredericksburg, and at dawn of the 29th of April it was started from its huts by the long roll upon the drum, which, mingling with the rattle of musketry, announced that "fighting Joe Hooker" was about to try his fortunes against Lee.

Wellington's foresight in studying the field of Waterloo a year before the battle gave him signal advantage over Napoleon. Jackson, with characteristic prudence, had studied the adjacent country

---

* Davis and Jackson, p. 276.

II

during the winter months, and was prepared to avail himself of
every tactical and strategic advantage over Hooker. It was a moment
that called forth every element of our generalship and soldiership.
Hooker, with 120,000 infantry and artillery, and 10,000 cavalry,
confronted Lee, who had only 45,000 infantry and artillery and
and a small force of cavalry.*

Hooker's plans soon developed. Leaving Sedgwick with 22,000
men at Fredericksburg, he crossed the Rappahannock at Kelly's
Ford, twenty-seven miles above, with the remainder, and appeared at
Chancellorsville, ten miles from Lee's left at Fredericksburg, on May
the 1st; and confident that his advantageous position would force
Lee to retreat, he announced to his army that "the enemy must
either ingloriously fly, or come out from behind his defences and give
us battle on our own ground, where certain destruction awaits him;"
and boastfully asserted amongst his officers and men that "the rebel
army is now the legitimate property of the Army of the Potomac."†

Leaving Early in the trenches at Fredericksburg with five brigades
of 7,500 bayonets to hold at bay his three-fold over-numerous foe,
Lee turned to Chancellorsville, and with 38,000 faced Hooker's
95,000. On the night of the 2d of May Jackson suggested an idea
which Lee immediately approved and adopted, and on the 3d it was
put in execution. Winding rapidly around Hooker's right flank
with Rodes', Colston's, and A. P. Hill's divisions, not quite 18,000
strong, Jackson gained the reverse of the Union lines by 5 o'clock in
the evening. Hooker's scouts had caught a glimpse of this column as
it passed his right flank, but that commander never divining its purpose, concluded that it was "ingloriously flying," and dispatched to
Sedgwick : "We know the enemy is flying, trying to save his trains."‡
It was near sunset. Scarcely a sound disturbed the solemn solitudes of
the wilderness, save, perhaps, a dried twig broke under the foot of
the startled deer§ that snuffed mischief in the evening breeze. The

---

* "General Longstreet, with two divisions of his corps, was detached for
service south of James River in February, and did not rejoin the army until
after the battle of Chancellorsville."—*Lee's Report.*

† Swinton : Army of the Potomac, p. 276.

‡ Swinton, p. 284. "It happened that the road along which Jackson's
column was filing bends somewhat southward, so that though the movement was discovered, it was misinterpreted as a retreat towards Richmond
on the part of Lee."

§ Deer were actually started up by our troops.

federal troops, apprehending no danger save from Lee in front, had thrown up earthworks to repel him, and with countenances smiling in conscious security and anticipated victory, were taking their evening meal. Suddenly there arose a deafening cheer, and the earth shook with the tramp of rushing lines and the thunder of cannon. The smoke clears away, and behold the wreck of a ruined host! A corps of 11,000 men had been shivered as by lightning. * The tide of victory was rising—the rout of Hooker had begun ; but stop! our leader—where is he?

> "They had fought like brave men, hard and well ;
> They had piled the ground with foemen slain ;
> They had conquered ; but their Jackson fell
> Bleeding at every vein."

It was alas too true! Filled with a sense of the momentous issues of the moment, and his whole soul aflame with the ardor of battle, Jackson had ridden in advance of his skirmish line preparatory to pushing forward his troops in vigorous pursuit. He had just decided where to strike, and had sent a courier with his last battle order : "Tell A. P. Hill to press right on." Turning to ride back, his own troops mistook him and his staff for federal cavalry and fired upon them. His right hand was pierced, and his left arm broken in two places. Several of his attendants were killed. With firm self-possession he reined his horse with his wounded hand, but presently fell fainting in the arms of his staff. They were accidentally joined in a few minutes by A. P. Hill and his aides. They were so near the enemy's lines that two skirmishers came up to the group around the stricken General and were captured. The blood was soon staunched, and he was placed upon a litter; but just at this time the rallying enemy and our advanced line came in contact, a tempest of grape-shot swept over them, one of the litter bearers was cut down and the General hurled violently to the earth.

Thus ended the story of Stonewall Jackson.

Where in the annals of our race can we find so touching a spectacle of the vanity of human hopes, and the frailty of human glory?

---

* "The 11th corps had been brushed way. * * * Jackson had seized the breastworks, had taken the whole line in reverse, pushed forward to within half-a-mile of head-quarters, and now proceeded to make preparations for following up his success by a blow that should be decisive."
—*Swinton*, p. 287.

Where shall we find so much glory compressed in a short time—where so sad and sudden a termination? Two years before an unknown colonel of artillery—now a great leader, whose every word was a harbinger of destiny—whose every act varied the drama of history. Twenty victories had culminated in this supreme exertion of his genius—the glories of Chancellorsville had risen upon the mingled glories of twenty fields.

> "Like another morn
> Risen upon midnoon."

The arm of the hero is raised to strike the final blow which is to make the sun of victory stand still! When lo! itself is struck, and the leader of hosts lies there upon the earth a feeble piece of bleeding clay, while the rush of feet is around him, and the pitiless battle hail robs him even of his gory bed.

They carried him from the field to the house of a friend, and all that love and skill could do was done for him. There were sad faces in the old Second Corps when the dreadful news was whispered along the lines that night, and down the powder and dust-stained cheek of many a veteran trickled the long unknown tear. "Jackson wounded!" They heard it with mingled incredulity and dread. They had seen him so often sitting upon his horse in the midst of fire and slaughter, with placid countenance, and hand upraised in prayer, that they knew him impregnable to fear—they had seen him so often come forth unscathed that they had begun to believe that he wore a charmed life impregnable to danger. But the truth was relentless. He had fallen. Would he live? Would he rise again and return to them after a season? These were the anxious questions now. Stuart was sent for and the next day his plume floated over their bayonets as they pierced the enemys ranks, and the cry mingled with their cheers, "charge and remember Jackson!" His name there, and in all their after battles fought with them—alas! it could not guide them.

For a few days Jackson lingered. His left arm had been amputated, and disease had supervened upon his wound. But he was cheerful and hopeful. He spoke with all affection of his officers and men, and expressed the opinion, which history must affirm, that had he not been wounded Hooker's Army would have been utterly annihilated. Yet with characteristic modesty he said of his movement "I expect to receive far more credit for it than I deserve. Most men will think I planned it from the first; but it was not so—I simply took advantage of circumstances as they were presented to me in the providence of God. I feel that his hand led me—let us give him all the glory." *

On the morning of the 10th of May, his wife who had come to attend him informed him that the Doctors said there was no hope—he must "soon be in heaven." He only answered "I prefer it, and I will be an infinite gainer 'to be translated.'" Did ever the parting soul meet the last enemy more nobly?

In his last hours his mind wandered—perhaps back to the battle-field: "tell A. P. Hill to prepare for action," he said. At another time "tell Major Hawks† to send forward provisions for the troops." Again "it is all right." In his last moments he murmured "let us pass over the river, and rest under the shade of the trees." Perhaps he saw again the green banks of the Shenandoah, perhaps he caught a glimpse of those "green pastures, and still waters" where the weary are at rest: and thus with resignation to the will of heaven, and anticipation of its joys, the soul of our great warrior passed away from us.‡

How like were his to the dying words of Arthur, the blameless King, as the Poet Laureate has rendered them :

"I am going a long way
To the Island valley of Avilion,
Where falls not hail, or rain, or any snow,
Nor ever wind blows loudly; but it lies
Deep meadowed, happy, fair with orchard lawns
And bowery hollows crowned with summer sea,
Where I will heal me of my grievous wound."

* Dr. Dabney's life of Jackson.
† His Commissary.
‡ I give Mr. Swinton's remarks, though not concurring in them.

"Thus died Stonewall Jackson the ablest of Lee's lieutenants. Jackson was essentially an executive officer, and in this sphere he was incomparable. Devoid of high mental parts, and destitute of that power of planning and combination, and of that calm broad military intellect, which distinguished General Lee whom he regarded with a child-like reverence, and whose designs he loved to carry out, he had yet those elements of character that, above all else, inspire troops. A fanatic in religion, fully believing he was destined by heaven to beat his enemy whenever he encountered him, he infused something of his own fervent faith into his men, and at the time of his death had trained a corps whose attacks in column were unique, and irresistible; and it was noticed that Lee ventured upon no strokes of auda-city after Jackson had passed away."—*Army of the Potomac, Swinton p. 290.*

Jackson was dead! It struck every Southerner like a bolt in the bosom. The great right arm of Lee that had been uplifted so often in prayer, and had descended so terribly, after gathering strength from heaven, was shattered—gone. Lee fought henceforth one armed.

Ewell, Early, and Gordon succeeded in turn to the command of the Second Corps. They were noble, heroic, and able generals, but it is no disparagement of either to say that neither filled the place vacated by Jackson. It is but just to them to add that neither had the opportunity.

From friend and foe alike came his praise. We can all join in the tribute paid him by our ex-President while a captive: "For glory," said he, "he had lived long enough, and if this result had to come it was the Divine mercy that removed him. He fell like the eagle, his own feather on the shaft that was dripping with his life blood. In his death the Confederacy lost an eye and an arm, our only consolation being that his summons could have reached no soldier more prepared to accept it joyfully."[*] Nor will we be lacking in esteem for the generous, patriotic, and christian spirit of the Northern editor who rose above the unholy passions which the war had aroused, and paid this tribute to the genius and character of Jackson:[†] "No other man has impressed the imagination of our soldiers and the community as much as he. An unknown name at the beginning of the war, save to his brother officers and his classes in the military school at Lexington, Virginia, his footsteps were earliest in the field from which now death has withdrawn him. But in two years he has made his name familiar in every civilized land on the globe as a general of rare skill, resource, and energy. No other general of the South could develope so much power out of slender and precarious means, by the fervid inspiration of his own mind, as Jackson. He had absolute control of his men, seeming almost to fascinate them. * * * Henceforth we know him no more after the flesh. He is no longer a foe. We think of him now as a noble-minded gentleman, a rare and eminent christian. For years he had been an active member of the Presbyterian church of which he was a ruling elder. He never, in all the occupations of the camp or temptations of campaigns, lost the fervor of his piety or remitted his christian duties. * * * Let no man suppose that the North will triumph

---

[*] Craven's Prison Life of Jefferson Davis.

[†] Letter to New York Independent, quoted in Doolady's sketch of Jackson, p. 248.

over a fallen son with insulting gratulations. No where else will the name of Jackson be more honored." We respect the author of such sentiments. Let the hates and resentments of the war perish with it. The time shall come when in either section there shall survive only admiration for what is best in each; and then from above the firesides of the American People the iron moulded countenance of Stonewall Jackson, and the benignant, patriarchal countenance of Robert Lee shall look down upon the rising generations.